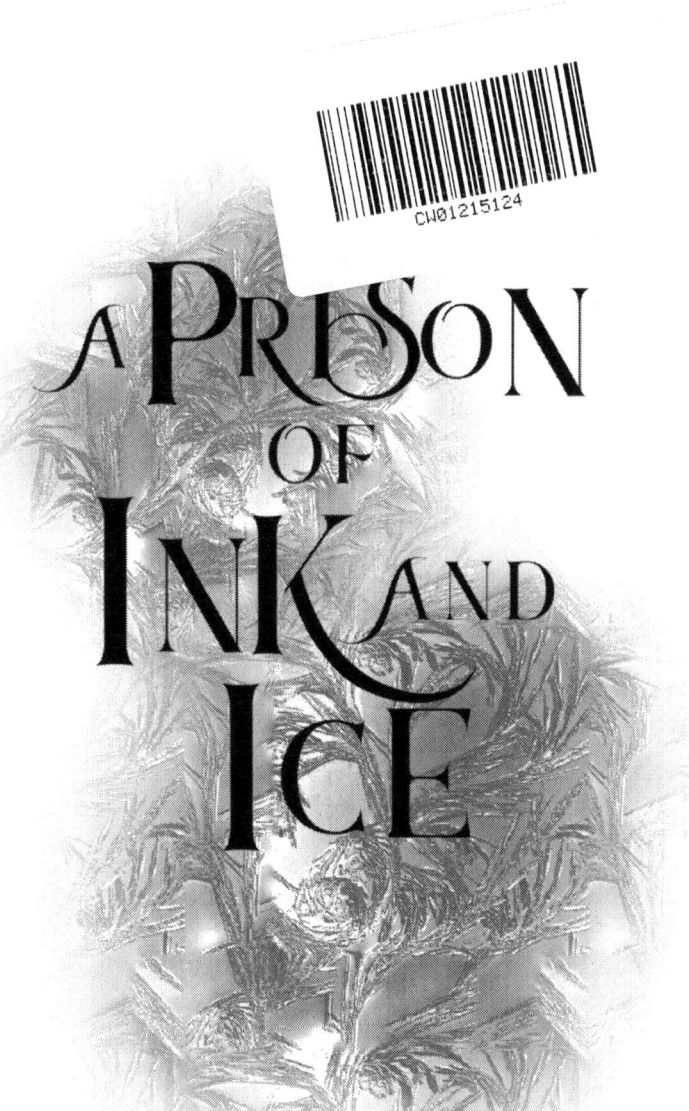

A Prison of Ink and Ice

REBECCA F. KENNEY

This book is a work of fiction. Names, characters, places, and incidents are the product of the author's imagination or are used fictitiously. Any resemblance to actual events, locales, or persons, living or dead, is coincidental.

Copyright © 2024 by Rebecca F. Kenney

All rights reserved. In accordance with the U.S. Copyright Act of 1976, the scanning, uploading, and electronic sharing of any part of this book without the permission of the publisher is unlawful piracy and theft of the author's intellectual property. If you would like to use material from the book (other than for review purposes), prior written permission must be obtained by contacting the publisher at rfkenney@gmail.com. Thank you for your support of the author's rights.

First Edition: February 2024

Kenney, Rebecca F.
A Prison of Ink and Ice / by Rebecca F. Kenney—First edition.

Cover design by: Cedric Vitangcol of Grafico Espacio (@designsby.ced)

PLAYLIST

"All the King's Horses" –Karmina

"Brittle" –Icon For Hire

"It Is What It Is" –Lifehouse

"on purpose" –Ni/Co

"King" –Lauren Aquilina

"Come to Your Senses" –Alexandra Shipp, Vanessa Hudgens

"Call Out My Name" –Kelly Clarkson

"LOUD" –Sofia Carson

"Youngblood" –5 Seconds of Summer

"What Was I Made For?" –Billie Eilish

"Tearin' Up My Heart" –*NSYNC

"Dreaming" –Tones And I

READING GUIDANCE

Contains spoilers for *A Court of Sugar and Spice* and *A Court of Hearts and Hunger*

Violence, eye horror, dubious consent, thoughts of cheating, public sex, very brief mention of child sexual abuse in the past, size play, pet play, dragon sex, breath play, death, violence, blood-drinking, Fae consumption of human flesh, magical (temporary) gender swap of a character

The depiction of ADHD stems from my own experience and is not intended to reflect the lived experience of everyone with this particular neurodivergence.

1

LOUISA

At first, I can't remember anything.

Not even my name.

It's the most frightening sensation in the world.

My cheek is pressed to rough ice, the granular kind that scratches and scours. I'm lying on my stomach. I can see my hand not far away, plump bruised fingers limply arched against the ice. There's a band of silver metal around my wrist, with a chain leading from it, disappearing somewhere beyond my line of vision.

I can't move yet. I hurt everywhere.

What happened to me?

I strain for words, for names. My sister's name and face come to me before my own. Clara. Brown eyes, brown hair, quietly pretty. An artist. My best friend since I was born.

My mind struggles, climbs, and finds my own name—Louisa.

Where am I?

This isn't… this isn't home… Although I'm not sure what home is anymore. My mind is divided there. I have glimpses of a stately house, neatly appointed, full of rigid rules. And then another building—a palace of slender columns and glossy hallways, of elaborate paintings and soft fragrances, of richly clad people with pointed ears.

Faerie. In Faerie, my home is the palace, because I'm… I'm married to…

His face enters my mind. Crisp, beautiful, regal. Clear pale skin, jet black hair. Green eyes. A sense of power beyond anything I've known—he's the most powerful being in this realm, in fact.

Lirannon. King of Faerie—or at least of the Seelie kingdom. My husband. My Chosen. My mate.

The word makes me cringe inside. I'm not sure why.

I shift against the ice, and immediately an ache floods my bones, but I push myself up anyway. My brain is beginning to awaken now, to leap from one detail to the next. Silly details, like the way the snowy, icy floor looks like frozen sugar. Like the way three of the metal bars in the window of my cell are fully coated with ice, and one is only half-covered.

I'm cold. Deathly cold and stiff, hurting and hungry, so hungry. How long was I lying unconscious on the floor of this cell? How did I get here?

"Think back, Louisa," I whisper to myself. "What's the last thing you remember?"

I close my eyes and pinch the bridge of my nose. It's as if my brain was frozen into a solid chunk, and now it's gradually thawing. But I don't want to wait for the full thaw, so I claw the memories out of the ice.

A prison... a prison... there's something in that. Lir and I were going to visit a prison. A prison where he'd placed Drosselmeyer's Unseelie victims until he could question them and see if it was safe to release them.

The prison was established by an ancestor of Lir's and fortified with magical safeguards. Lir told me it was full of devices designed to suppress magic, that the cells themselves were laced with iron and silver to keep the Fae prisoners sick and subservient. It sounded rather barbaric to me at the time, but then he told me the crimes of some of the captives, and I felt less sorry for them. I can't remember the specifics of the stories now, only the feeling of horror.

So we were going to the prison... Griem Dorcha, it was called. It was one of the stops on our goodwill tour through Faerie, to get everyone used to the idea of having a human queen. I knew it would be a rather stressful trip, full of surprises, but I assumed Lir and I would have some fun, too. Since the defeat of the Rat King, he's been so busy driving out the Unseelie monsters and stabilizing the kingdom that I've barely seen him. Any fucking we do is quick and quiet. I want it loud and long and adventurous.

I remember riding in the carriage with Lir. On the first day of our trip, he got out his lap desk and busied himself with huge ledgers and stacks of documents while I read a book and drank wine. The second day, sometime in the afternoon, I wanted to have a little fun in the carriage, maybe suck his cock or have him eat me out, but he said that would be inappropriate. Then he got out the lap desk again, while I sulked in the corner of the coach. He kept stealing glances at me, tried to persuade me to read or sew or something, but I didn't want to. I fetched my short sword from beneath the bench seat of the carriage and polished it for a while, but I soon grew tired of that.

And then I said something petulant, something I regretted instantly. "Captain Dónal would let me suck his dick if we were traveling together."

Captain Dónal is rather a sore point with Lir. Dónal is a tall, tanned Fae with a mane of snow-white curls and a pair of vivid blue eyes. When he's training shirtless, as he often does, his skin gleams like molten bronze. He's been one of my regular trainers ever since Lir took back the throne, and I've learned much from him. I won't deny that occasionally, when we're training, I've been wet with more than sweat. I'm only human—I can't be expected to be perfectly immune to the charms of a magnificent Fae warrior. But I've never sought satisfaction from Dónal, only from Lir.

When I made that comment in the carriage, though, Lir turned salt-white and his green eyes grew absolutely venomous. I believe if Dónal had been anywhere around, Lir would have killed him on the spot.

Wicked thing that I am, I loved inciting that jealousy in him. I would have pushed him further, but then something happened...

Something I can't remember. Something that interrupted our journey.

We were close to the prison—I remember that much. We would have reached it by nightfall.

I can't remember if we did.

Maybe that's where I am now—the great Seelie prison of Griem Dorcha. But if so, why am I chained in a cell like a prisoner? Did Lir put me here? If he did, there must have been a good reason. He wouldn't do that unless...

Unless I did something truly terrible.

Maybe I fucked someone else? One of our guards? He told me once that if I grew tired of him and wanted pleasure elsewhere, he wouldn't deny me that choice; but perhaps the reality of it was too much for him to handle and he flew into a jealous rage.

No, that doesn't sound like him. He may be maddening at times, but he is *good*. Noble. Kind. A true king in every sense of the word.

He's so much better and nobler and kinder than me. Sometimes I wonder if he regrets choosing me.

Sometimes I wonder if...

But I stop myself on the brink of that thought, because beyond it lies a gaping chasm I'm not ready to face.

I prop myself against the cold wall of the cell. The rock is filmed with ice, yet when I lean against it, the ice doesn't melt— not in the slightest. My fingers aren't even wet.

There's something uncanny about this ice, this prison.

The door of the cell blends into the wall so well it's barely visible. Before I can even think about trying to open it, I need to get rid of my shackle and chain.

I've just begun tugging on the chain in earnest when something bangs outside the cell, like a door closing at the end of a very long hallway.

I hurry toward the door of my cell, but I can't quite reach it before the length of my chain pulls me up short.

There's a slow, scraping sound, like something being dragged along snow-crusted ice. The sound halts right outside my cell, and after a few seconds, the door swings open.

The figure standing in the hallway is that of a naked woman, heavy-breasted, with thick, strong legs. Her body is twined with black chains and strips of blood-soaked fur, and she has the head of an enormous, shaggy, black-furred ox. I can't tell if it's a mask, a curse, or her natural form. The space between her legs is cloaked with matted black curls, and smears of dark blood decorate her bare arms and legs. In one hand she grips a long whip of jointed metal shards, fused together. There's blood on the whip, too, and bits of soggy hair.

The eyes of the ox are glossy black, except for the glint of two snowflakes, one on the surface of each eye. They're not melting, just clinging there, right over her irises. Strange.

In the pale gray light leaking between the bars of the window, she looks both nightmarish and oddly out of place.

"Where am I?" I manage to ask through chilled lips.

"In the prison of Griem Dorcha." Her voice is low, thick, and animalistic, and the muzzle of the ox head moves as if she's speaking with its jaws and tongue. "Under the protection of the Banríon."

"Protection?" I glance at the shackle on my wrist.

"The Banríon is the protector of all."

"Right, well, I'm Louisa, Queen of the Seelie, wife of Lirannon the High King, and I demand to know where my husband is."

The ox-woman snorts, but it's not really a sound of contempt—more like surprise or confusion. "You remember?"

"Remember what?"

"Who you are. You remember who you are?"

"Of course I do."

The great black ox-head begins to sway back and forth. "No, no, no. This is wrong, and they will be angry. They will be angry with *me*. No, no, no, you must pretend that you do not remember."

"Pretend?"

"Yes! I am to take you to court, and you must pretend you remember nothing, or the Banríon will kill us both."

"I thought the Banrion was the protector of all?"

"Yes, all," repeats the ox-woman. "All who *obey*."

"So you want me to pretend that my memory is gone? That I don't know who I am or where I came from?"

"Yes, pretend. Pretend to have forgotten," moans the ox-woman. "It's better that way, for me, for you, for all of us. Pretend, and be quiet."

"I'm not usually quiet, whether I remember things or not," I mutter. "But I'll try. Who are you, anyway?"

"I do not remember. No one does," she replies. "I live below. I guard the new ones until they are ready to become pets or guests of the Banrion. Their minds are usually empty, simple. Yours is full. Not good. The Banrion already despises me. She will kill me, kill me... it's best to kill you now, before she finds out..." Her throaty voice rises to a bellowing moan, and I hurry to placate her.

"I already said I'll be quiet," I say. "I'll pretend to have lost my memory. You won't be in any danger."

The ox-woman swings her head a few more times, but she seems to be settling down.

"What about the others that were with me?" I ask. "A tall Fae with black hair and green eyes? And there were royal guards with us."

"Forget them." The ox-woman licks her muzzle with a broad tongue, cleaning away a trace of blood. "One was eaten already. The rest are for later."

Shit. Oh, shit.

I try to express my horror, but the words won't come. Just as well, because she might decide to kill me after all.

When I don't respond, she trudges forward and unbolts the end of my chain from the wall. "Come. The Banrion will summon the pets soon, both new and old. We must wash you, change you."

Until now I've been so distracted by the cold that I didn't notice what I was wearing or what state it was in. But as the ox-woman speaks, I realize that I'm still in my traveling clothes and—gods help me—I think I've pissed myself at least once. How long was I lying unconscious in this room?

A wash and a change of clothes are a *need*, not a want, and then afterwards I can visit this Banrion person and figure out what the fuck is going on. We're at the prison, that much is clear—and it also seems clear that the place is under new management. But how were we taken captive? How did the Banrion overcome Lir's incredible magic?

What if he is the one who was "eaten already," as the ox-woman said?

No, it can't be. If he were dead, I would have felt it. We are bound, he and I—Chosen mates after the tradition of the Seelie royals. I would know if he had disappeared from the world.

He has to be alive. His death is not an option I'm willing to accept.

The ox-woman takes me to a bare stone room with a copper tub. She watches and grunts with impatience while I bathe in the steaming water. Once I'm done and wrapped in a towel, she takes me to a stone stairway with a gate at its foot.

A tall, lovely Fae stands there, waiting to receive me. Snowflakes gleam in her eyes, too, but they're only visible at certain angles—as she looks down to unlock the gate, they disappear.

She opens the gate long enough to let me pass, then bolts it again with a scornful look at the ox-woman. With a grunt, the ox-woman turns and trudges back into the darkness, dragging her jointed whip behind her.

"So you're one of the new arrivals," says the Fae with a disdainful curl of her lip. "A *human*. We only have a few of those here. You'll need this." She clasps a golden bracelet around my wrist. "It will help regulate your body temperature. You'll feel the cold, but it won't be as severe. Come, we must get you dressed for Court. And *hurry*. The others are almost ready."

2

LOUISA

A short time later, I'm lined up with eleven other "pets." That's what we're being called by the Fae servants who are bustling around us, fixing our outfits and our hair. There are nine other Fae and two humans, none of whom I recognize, and all of whom seem vaguely blissful and contented, eager for whatever's about to happen.

The wide hallway we're standing in is cloaked with ice, and though I'm chilly, I'm nowhere near as cold as I was in that cell. The bracelet must be working.

Besides the bracelet, my outfit consists of a fur bustier and white doeskin panties, also fur-trimmed. I don't like thinking about the animals who perished to provide the outfit, but I wasn't given a choice of clothing.

My breasts barely fit into the bustier, and my belly is exposed in all its heavy roundness. I usually prefer corsets or gowns that support my breasts better and hold my stomach in a bit. Not that I'm ashamed of how I look—I'm just more comfortable that way. More secure. Nevertheless, I love myself, from the swell of my stomach to the breadth of my hips, and I'm determined to own this outfit.

This body is more than beautiful, it's powerful. I've been training for a few months now, and I've become much better with a sword. Dónal has taught me how to use my weight to my advantage in hand-to-hand combat as well. And I will, when I need to. But I have to gather more information first.

Someone Unseelie is definitely in charge of this prison, and from Clara's stories of the Rat King's Court, I know the sort of entertainment that usually occurs in the domains of Unseelie rulers. As Finias would remind me, not all the Unseelie are wicked, but many of them enjoy dark pastimes, like slow torture, rape, devouring the flesh of Fae or humans, and a variety of other atrocities. The fact that all twelve of us in this lineup are being called "pets" and trotted out in scanty clothing doesn't bode well for the upcoming activities. But I'm determined to survive, no matter what I have to do. I'll fuck whoever I need to, charm them if I can, do anything it takes to make it through the day, or night—I'm not sure what time it is. I can handle forced sex and kink, up to a point, without breaking. My greater fear is that someone will decide my full-fleshed body looks extra delicious and decide to partake in a more devastating way. I definitely prefer being eaten out to being *eaten*.

"You there." A Fae attendant snaps her fingers in front of my face. "Move."

I shuffle after the others, who are moving toward a pair of tall, ice-covered doors that stand partway open. I got lost in my thoughts just now, like I sometimes do. It usually happens when I have to wait for something, or when I have to do a chore I don't particularly like. I'm not fond of switching from one task to the next, either—once I'm deeply involved in a thing, I'd rather stay with it than change course to something else—

Gods, I'm doing it again. Wandering in my head when I need to stay focused, stay alert.

One of the attendants speaks to all of us as we file through the doors. "Go straight up to the Banríon's mirror and stand along its edge. The Favorite will choose one or more of you to entertain everyone tonight."

So it is night. And we are the entertainment. I heard nothing that sounded cannibalistic, which is promising. Although one never knows in Faerie.

The room we're ushered into must have once been a dining hall for the prison, or perhaps a common area. The ceilings are at least three stories high. The stone arches and peaks far above me are glazed with ice, and icicles hang from them in crystalline clusters, like frozen chandeliers. Some of the clusters actually glow with a rich light, like the sun shining through ice. The frozen walls are faintly blue, patterned in frosty swirls. Four tiers of benches, all made of ice, run the length of the room on both sides.

On the benches, seated upon furs and white doeskins, a motley crowd of Fae has gathered. Some have the heads of deer or bulls, like the woman who came to fetch me from my cell. Some have crystal wings laced with shining opalescent veins, while others boast huge feathered wings or white antlers. Others are serpentine, their lower halves sinuous, encased in glossy white scales.

Though most of the onlookers are dressed in simple garb, I spot a few familiar items—some of my gowns and Lir's outfits, the cloaks and doublets of our royal guards, a scattering of the royal jewels on strangers' fingers, ears, and throats. I swallow the protest that rises on my lips and try to keep my face blank.

In the center of the immense chamber lies a sheet of silver ice, as flat and reflective as a mirror. From its surface rises an enormous throne, all frosted spines and pointed peaks and pale branching antlers.

The Fae female on the throne is possibly the most beautiful woman I've ever seen. She has dainty pointed ears rimmed with sparkling icicles. Her smooth skin matches the pale blue of the icy walls. Her white hair is pulled tightly back from her face. On her head sits a delicate crown of silver, with ice crystals in place of gemstones.

I'm momentarily stunned by her flawless features and her full lavender lips. She has a graceful neck, slender arms, and elegant fingers tipped with icy claws. Her gown surprises me, though—snow-white brocade for the bodice, but starting at the waist it flares into a sea of purple flowers, their petals lightly frosted.

This must be the Banríon.

And at her feet, draped on white cushions, reclines Lir.

My heart quivers and leaps.

His lean, toned body is paler than usual, and he wears only an undergarment of black silk, slung low on his hips. Several delicate necklaces of ice and crystal decorate his chest, and a collar of frost coats his neck from collarbones to chin.

He's so fucking beautiful.

I stumble against the pet in front of me, a thickly built male Fae with green skin. He turns and hisses at me.

"Apologies," I whisper.

Before he turns away, I spot a pale snowflake overlaying each of his eyes, too. There for a second, and then gone.

I twist around to look at the female Fae behind me. At first I don't see anything in her eyes, but when I angle my head a bit, I spot the same oddity—a pair of large snowflakes, one in each of her eyes.

Self-consciously I blink, wondering if my eyes look the same. Or perhaps these strange snowflakes are the side-effect of a memory spell.

As we line up at the edge of the immense mirror of ice, I lean forward, peering down the row of pets to see if I can spot the same thing in anyone else's eyes. But I'm not close enough, so I turn my attention back toward the throne. My heart is pounding so loudly I'm sure the Fae around me can hear it.

The Banríon extends her hand to Lir and murmurs something. He takes her fingers and kisses her knuckles lightly, tenderly. Then he rises, unfolding his long body, and approaches the line of pets, his narrow feet treading confidently on the glassy ice. There's a sparkling bit of jewelry around his left ankle and a silver ring on one toe. Silly things to notice, I suppose, but they're unlike him, and that hurts. He doesn't wear jewelry on his ankles or feet, ever.

From somewhere off to the right, a voice intones, "As you all know, the former Favorite is unfortunately deceased. But our Lady has chosen a new Favorite for tonight's festivities. He will now select his playmate for the evening."

Lir. *Lir* is the new "Favorite" of the Banríon. My husband is going to choose someone to… *play with*.

He would never willingly dress like this in front of others. He's always proper, always fully clothed when he appears in public. And he has power, so much power. Magic that could decimate this room, this entire prison. If he had full control of it, he would have used it by now. He would have come for me hours ago and killed everyone in his path.

But he hasn't. Which means he's not himself. The memory spell must have worked on him—there's no other way to explain this. No other reason he would be kissing the hand of the Banríon and selecting a "playmate for the evening."

The Banríon must be able to wield both the powers of memory and of ice. I've been told that Fae don't possess the power to actually *create* water, except in a few cases; but she must be one of those rare cases, judging by the sheer quantity of ice in this fortress. She's responsible for the transformation of this prison into a cage of devastating beauty.

As if to prove my point, she produces several slim shards of ice from her fingers and makes them spin and rotate in midair above her palm.

She's dangerous, that much is clear. Does she know who we are? That Lir is king of the Seelie? She must know. We were in royal garb, in a royal coach, surrounded by royal guards. Lir was wearing a fucking crown, for gods' sake.

He's certainly not wearing it now. And as he draws nearer, I spot the glint of something in his eyes. Maybe snowflakes. He's still too far away for me to be sure.

I want to call out to him, but I manage to hold my tongue. Best to follow the ox-woman's advice and stay silent until I figure out what's going on.

Lir begins at one end of the line and paces slowly along, surveying each candidate. When he reaches out and touches the cheek of a Fae woman, I bite my lip so hard I taste blood.

Blood. Why didn't I think of that sooner? My blood released him from Drosselmeyer's curse. Perhaps it can free him from this spell and restore his memories. I just have to get him to choose me, to kiss me.

But if he truly doesn't know who I am, and I have to pretend we're strangers, how can I make him choose me?

I shouldn't be worried—I've seduced dozens of people in my lifetime, and I charmed Lir once. I can do it again.

But the memories of how I tried to seduce him—how I stripped in front of him, played with myself while he watched, grabbed his cock while we hid in a closet—they're not pleasant. They each come with the sting of rejection, and with the horrible feeling that I went too far. My nerves, the insecurity of being in a new world, my need for comfort, for conquest—it's an explanation for the way I pushed him, but not an excuse.

So when he steps in front of me and looks down into my face, I can't bring myself to do it again. None of it. I don't smirk and simper, or arch a brow at him, or strike a seductive pose. I simply stand before him and look into those familiar green eyes.

I see *him* in those eyes, but I'm not there. I don't see the tiniest hint of recognition, the slightest remembrance of our history, the months we've spent together. All I see is the calm, casual interest of a stranger.

There is no possible way he could be faking forgetfulness—not like this. His cousin Fin is the trickster, the actor—not Lir. He truly doesn't remember me. And it has something to do with the twin snowflakes shining in his eyes.

I was so angry with him on the way here, and now I feel like crying. Like collapsing into a melted mess at his feet. But that's not how I do things. Clara and I—we've always stood firm together against whatever came our way. We cried rarely, and never in public.

I pretend she's beside me. I fight the tears, and I hold Lir's gaze.

He leans in, inhaling through his nose.

Godstars... my *scent*. I still have the special scent that marks me as his Chosen. Even if he has forgotten me, my fragrance calls to him. Maybe that will be enough for him to select me as his playmate…

But he's moving away. Cupping the chin of the Fae next to me.

I release a long, shaky breath as Lir continues on down the line. Tears sting my eyes.

Wait…

He's coming back. Stepping into my space, his eyes roving over my breasts, my belly, my thighs. He's surveying the generous proportions of me, swelled even further in recent months by the rich food of Faerie. I happen to enjoy cake even more than I like training.

"Beautiful," he murmurs. Then louder he announces, "This one."

3

LIR

There is no before, there is only now.
There is no future, there is only the present.
There is no pain, only pleasure.
There is no purpose except to serve the Banríon.

Those words echo faintly in my head now and then, in a cool female voice. Like a soothing refrain, the chant settles my mind every time my thoughts start to spin too quickly.

There's relief in that voice. Delight in yielding to it.

I care for the Banríon. Not as a lover—she made it clear to me that she and I would not couple. But I am grateful to her for providing this beautiful fortress in which to serve her, and for giving me a locus for my otherwise useless life.

Because I care, and because I am grateful, I do as she asks.

Tonight, I will serve her by playing with one of the other pets. I am the Favorite, so I may choose my partner—or partners, if I want more than one. Once I make my selection, the Court and the Banríon will watch us couple on the soft pillows laid upon our Lady's mirror. She calls it "The Mirror of Reason."

I have in my mind the knowledge of how to join with someone physically, but I don't think I have ever done it. Or perhaps I have. There are images in my head, cloudy and indistinct, but I can't quite grasp them.

There is no before, there is only now.
There is no future, there is only the present.
There is no pain, only pleasure.
There is no purpose except to serve the Banríon.

My body relaxes. No need to be concerned. I know what to do, and everything will be clear and perfect as long as my intent is to please the Lady.

"You please me best by pleasing yourself," she told me quietly, before we came to this great hall. "Choose the partner who delights your eye and tempts your body."

The girl I have chosen is human. I have some rudimentary knowledge of humans, but I am not sure if I have encountered one before.

There is no before, there is only now.

This girl is beautiful beyond imagination. Voluptuous and charming, with a pair of intelligent blue eyes and a round, rosy mouth. There's a carnal richness about her figure that floods my head with filthy images of what I could do to her.

But there's something else about her, too—a fragrance. Like warm, syrupy, sugared fruit. Like delicate nectar from the daintiest flowers. Like running water, foamy and refreshing. There are so many layers to that scent—I think I could spend all night enjoying them.

I lead the girl onto the spread of thick furs and white pillows that have been laid upon the mirror, not far from the throne. The Banríon told me all the participants in this game are fully consenting—willing to serve, as I am. We are one in our desire to find and give pleasure.

The pet and I stand there, face to face, and I begin to shift and unfasten the clothing she wears. I can already see the lovely swell of her stomach, the dimpled texture of her thighs, the little dents in her plump knees. But I'm desperate to see her whole body. And I need to be closer to the source of that intoxicating scent. Perhaps it will be strongest upon her lips, along her cleavage, or deep between her legs. I'll explore each of those places thoroughly.

The girl shivers as I gently strip away her coverings.

She's staring at me. She doesn't look eager for this. She looks—sad.

"Are you cold?" I murmur.

She sucks in a little gasp as if my voice hurt her.

"Not really," she says, low. "They gave me this, to help keep me warm." She holds up one arm, graced with a bracelet.

"Very good." I smile, sliding my fingers along her upper arms to get her used to my touch. "Are you ready to join with me?"

"I... yes." She bites her lip, and a dot of blood appears on it. "But first, tell me your name."

"I am the Favorite."

"Yes, but surely you have a name."

"I do?"

"Everyone does."

"The Banríon calls me Raven sometimes."

"That's a pet name, not a real name."

A voice glides from the throne, across the icy mirror. "Is something the matter, my pets?"

"Of course not," says the girl with a bright smile, first at the Banríon, then at me. "Kiss me, Favorite."

She tips up her round, lovely face and I bend to greet her mouth with mine.

She introduces her tongue immediately, slipping through my lips and painting the inside of my mouth with the flavor of her blood. I'm immobilized, shocked by the sweet, sensual heat trickling along my throat, through my body. My cock hardens still more.

The girl pulls back, eyeing me intently. Like she expects some reaction to the taste of her blood.

"Mmm," I murmur, gathering her glorious body against mine.

"Your name?" she whispers, so quietly I barely hear it.

My name. She seems to want it desperately, and I feel a sense of loss that I cannot give her what she desires. But I will give her something equally satisfying.

"Lie down," I urge. "Forget names, and let me taste you."

Her eyes fill with pain and disappointment. Only for a second, though, and then she reaches up, wraps her arms around my neck, and murmurs, "Yes, you can taste me. You can fuck me and use me before all these Fae. I am yours, always."

Always? That sounds as if she expects this tryst of ours to be repeated in the future.

The cool voice in my head brings me up short, seals away those intrusive thoughts. *There is no future, there is only the present.*

The golden-haired girl reclines on the furs and pillows, in the center of the mirror of ice. I take a moment to admire how she looks lying there, with her thick, creamy thighs spread, and the plump lips of her sex on display. They're shining wet. She's aroused. Wants me. Wants *this*.

And her scent—it's stronger now, richer. I'm practically salivating for a taste.

I'm barely aware that anyone else exists as I drop to my knees and prostrate myself between the girl's arched knees.

The first lick across her pussy sends a thrill of groan-inducing ecstasy right to my cock, and it bobs beneath the silken fabric I'm wearing. She tastes like the warm sun and fresh-blooming flowers, like the richest food and the most divine liquor.

I slide my tongue over the two thick lips of her sex, caressing the thin, pink layers between them. Deeper I explore, into the sensitive heat of her slit, then up to the peak at the top. That little peak is flushed, swollen, tender.

Somehow, I know what to do. I understand how I'm supposed to cherish that tender bit of flesh, how I should bathe her pussy thoroughly, how I should open my mouth over her whole sex and pulse my tongue into her opening, over and over. How I should nip and stroke and tease her clit until she writhes with craving.

Now and then I pause to inhale, to relish the intricate fragrance of her.

As she grows more breathless and squirms more desperately, I eat her out more heartily, careful not to hurt her with my sharp canine teeth. Whoever she is, my chosen playmate for the evening deserves all the pleasure I can deliver, and not a drop of pain… unless she desires it.

4

LOUISA

Lir spends a long time with his face between my legs. At first I put on a bit of a show for the onlookers, moaning prettily, arching my back, fondling my huge tits. But even if he has lost his conscious memory, Lir's mouth and tongue remember their skill, and soon I'm not faking my reactions at all. I'm flushed, writhing, whimpering, so desperate for his cock that finally I push him away and get on all fours, ass up. The position is a plea in itself.

I hear the faint swish of him removing his flimsy undergarment. Then his strong hands, so familiar, grasp my ass cheeks and pull them apart. I curve my spine, sinking my body lower and raising my rear higher.

His cock head nudges at my entrance, probing my oversensitized pussy lips until I tremble and moan. I turn my head slightly, eyeing the Fae in the tiered seats. This is nothing like the orgy Clara described in the Rat King's court. These onlookers are mostly silent, with only soft gasps and faint moans belying their arousal. Most of them are still dressed, with their hands wriggling or jerking between their legs. Others are quietly coupling, their partially clothed bodies rocking slowly against each other.

The Banríon sits motionless, her hands clasping the arms of her throne. She's leaning forward slightly, watching us with keen intensity.

I turn away from her, from all of them, and I face down, toward the white fur covering the ice. Lir is still teasing me, caressing my bottom, squeezing it, bumping the tip of his warm cock against my slit.

I'm soaked. Melting. Shaking with need.

"Take me," I beg. "Fuck me, please, please, by the godstars, L—" I bite my tongue to keep from saying his name.

"Patience." His cock is burning hot, thick and hard, squeezing inside me with infuriating slowness.

I squeal with frustration, scrunching my fingers into the fur, almost crying. "Just fuck me already, fuck me like the naughty pet I am. Fuck me like you're punishing me."

"I said, *patience.*" He seizes a fistful of my hair and yanks my head back, while at the same moment slamming in.

My pulse skitters and I gasp.

Lir used to drink my blood. He was rather addicted to it, in fact. But he gave it up once his nutcracker curse was broken. Said it was an Unseelie practice, too dangerous, and that such things were beneath him. To be honest, I've missed it—the primal, visceral need he showed for me in those moments. Since we married, he gives me glimpses of *that* Lir, but he's always so controlled. So careful. Says he doesn't want to hurt me.

But in this moment, he doesn't know me, nor does he care if I get hurt. And I realize, with a flutter of frightened excitement, what that means.

It means I'm about to see Lir, unfettered.

Lir, released from all the pressures of court life and his own expectations of himself. Lir, without any memory of his father and his upbringing, without any of the responsibilities that weigh on him wherever he goes.

Without realizing it, this perverted ice queen has given me the exact thing I craved—to see my husband the king lose control more completely than he ever has before.

The kindling is set, soaked with oil. All I need is a match.

"I'm not patient," I tell him, with a backward lunge of my ass onto his cock, driving him deeper. "And I'm not obedient."

Lir laughs darkly. He's sunk to the hilt in me now, and he leans over my back, bringing his mouth close to my ear. One of his hands still grips my hair, keeping my head up, while his other hand slides across the front of my neck.

"Would you like me to teach you how to obey, pet?" he says softly.

I swallow, my throat moving against his hand. "Yes."

Lir's fingers tighten, restricting my breath. The ferocity of his grip on my hair and my throat is accompanied by the punishing slam of his hips into my ass, over and over. His cock pumps through me until I'm rocking on the edge of orgasm, my lungs swelling, my eyes rolled up, and the blood pooling in my face—I can't breathe—

His hand drops from my throat, and he pulls out of my pussy. I gasp for air.

Lir stalks around to my front and surveys me. I'm still on hands and knees, my belly swaying and my breasts trembling as I suck in breath after shattered breath.

He crouches, his erect cock jutting between his thighs, and he tips my face up. "You're human, and I don't want to hurt you beyond your capacity. If you can't bear what I'm doing to you, touch your ear like this." He taps his own. "And I'll stop."

I nod. Tears are gathering at the corners of my eyes, because we're in so much danger, and yet this is what I've always craved from him, and why, *why* couldn't he give it to me before? It hurts me that he can't let himself go like this without being robbed of all his memories.

He grabs my chin, jerks my face up, and forces my jaws open. Then he pushes his long cock over my tongue and down my throat so far that I gag. When he pulls back a little, I adjust my head, relaxing my throat to better accommodate him.

My pussy is still swollen, tingling, and hot, dripping with unfulfilled need. He's teaching me patience. The most delightful kind of lesson.

I circle the base of his cock with my hand and look up while I suck him, meeting those green eyes, so familiar, yet branded with the mark of the icy queen who's watching us. When I cast her a quick sidelong glance, I notice she still isn't touching herself. Strange. Usually people like to indulge in their own pleasure while they watch others fucking. She doesn't seem unaffected exactly, but she looks more intrigued than aroused.

Returning my attention to Lir, I see a telltale flush in my husband's pale cheeks. His color always heightens right before he comes.

He's so beautiful like this. I suck faster, taking him deeper, urging him to come for me, all the while drinking in the toned elegance of his form, his strong collarbones, broad shoulders—

And then I see the scar on his upper arm. The mark he will always carry, where a splinter broke off him while he was in nutcracker form.

The memory is too poignant—I can't stop the tears this time. I slide both hands around to his ass and press him closer, taking his cock deeper than I ever have, gagging myself on him while I weep silently. He comes with a soft male groan, plunging his hands into my hair.

Drawing back, I swallow every bit of his cum, and I lick him clean. He's panting, his lean stomach tightening, a rosy flush highlighting his cheekbones. Meanwhile I'm still aching for fullness, for *him*.

He's Fae. He can get hard again almost at once. I hope to the godstars he's going to keep fucking me. He can't leave me unsatisfied like this.

Lir reaches down, cups my chin. Drags his thumb across my wet lips, holding my gaze. Then he picks up his discarded bit of silken clothing and uses it to wipe the tears from my cheeks. "Good girl," he murmurs. "You drank my cum so fucking well."

My jaw nearly drops. Lir never speaks like that, not even when we're alone.

"It's my turn," I tell him. "I think I've been patient enough."

He laughs and arches a black brow. "That's for me to decide. Put your cheek to the fur, and raise that big, beautiful ass as high as you can. Let everyone see that gorgeous pussy, how it's quivering for my cock."

If he were in his right mind, he wouldn't do this. Wouldn't put me on display before others. He likes to keep me for himself. Although maybe that isn't so much his personal inclination as it is his upbringing. He told me once that his father kept sex very private, despised anything too adventurous in the bedroom, and rarely allowed even the most tame and tasteful of orgies at court. According to Lir, the former king was very disappointed in his nephew Finias for being so open and free with sex, as well as consorting with the Unseelie. Their disagreement ended in Fin being banished from Court entirely.

I wonder if the former king's attitude had a deeper impact on Lir than I realized. Perhaps Lir would be more open and permissive about sexual things if his father hadn't lectured him for decades on how such matters should be handled. In that respect, I suppose he and I are not so different. Both of us were raised with certain expectations. But I rebelled, while he bowed to them.

My husband certainly isn't prudish now. He walks around to my rear, grasps my ass cheeks, and opens me wider for the benefit of the onlookers. Then he trails two fingers through my wet pussy lips, stroking me over and over until I want to scream.

"Please," I mumble against the furs. "Please.

Lir pats my sex with his palm. "What do you think, my Lady?" he says to the Banríon. "Should I let her come?"

The Banríon doesn't reply, but there's an eager hiss of "yes" from the audience.

Lir positions himself at my backside again. He lays his cock between my ass cheeks and rubs it through that groove several times until I feel him hardening again, thickening. Then he tucks himself inside me and begins to fuck me with such punishing force that I squeal.

"I'm not going to touch your clit again," he says between thrusts. "You're going to come from my cock alone, like an obedient pet."

"Yes," I sob. "Oh yes... gods... *Lir*..."

Fuck, I'm coming, ecstasy jolting through my clit, through my whole body. But I made a mistake. I said his name when I came. I'm so used to saying it in moments of bliss.

He doesn't seem to have noticed, though. As he reaches his own climax, he cries out—a heavy, urgent, broken sound. I can feel the rhythm of his cock pulsing inside me.

And then it hits—a second wave of crashing, mind-bending, world-shattering pleasure. Our mate bond, flooding us both with an extra surge of orgasmic bliss. I scream with the soaring joy of it—it's almost too much to bear. And it's even more intense than usual, perhaps because Lir took his time and tried something new instead of simply laying me down, fucking me or eating me out, and being done with it.

I suppose that isn't fair to him. He was absent for a long time during his captivity with Drosselmeyer, and during that absence the Unseelie tore this land apart. Since Lir returned, he has been burdened with the business of driving out the enemy, rebuilding the kingdom, and regaining the trust of his people.

I told myself that I understood, that I was fine with it, that I was having better orgasms than I ever did before I met him, and that should be enough.

Still, his distraction hurt me, worse than I realized until right now, when I truly grasp what I've been missing. When the keen shearing ecstasy nearly makes me black out.

Lir's breath is ragged. He draws his cock out of me slowly. Then he pulls me to my feet, turns me around, and holds me against his body, face to face, while I tremble with the aftershocks of that incredible climax. It's almost like he's shielding me from everyone, letting me recover while the orgasmic sighs and gasps of the onlookers echo around us.

I set my forehead against Lir's chest, and I fight the oncoming surge of hot tears.

He chose me. We're still connected somehow, even though he doesn't know who I am. But what is that connection based on? Is it fate? Magic? A scent? Am I simply the body type he likes, or the style of beauty he prefers?

If it's not some surface attraction, it must be fate. I hate that option because that would mean we have no choice in the matter—even though Lir told me we did. He said we could accept the Chosen bond, or not. But he never told me what would happen if we accepted it, and then changed our minds.

He once promised he would let me seek pleasure with someone else if I wanted to, but he never mentioned dissolving the bond. Is it permanent? Unbreakable, even if I have second thoughts? If I *want* to change my mind?

Would I break it, if I could?

The pleasure we enjoy together is intense, yes... but amazing sex isn't enough reason for two people to stay married, is it? I feel as if we crashed together, hard and fast, and then drifted apart just as quickly.

Lir is gently pushing me away. Giving me a nod, his eyes bright. "That was most satisfying. Thank you for playing with me tonight."

"Oh... I... thank you for choosing me." The words cut my heart as I speak them. Little slivers of pain.

Hatred for the one who did this to us roars up in my chest, and I turn my head, intending to give the queen a glare as icy as her domain. But her throne is empty. Instead, there's a servant approaching me swiftly, walking carefully across the mirror of ice, carrying a robe of white fur.

"Come with me, please." The servant wraps the robe around my body. "The Banríon would like to speak with you."

5

LOUISA

I'm ushered down a narrow hallway and into a room that was probably the living quarters of the prison's commander. The furniture I can see beneath the layers of swirled frost seems of decent quality.

The Banríon stands near the end of the large canopy bed, which is festooned with icicles instead of curtains. She gestures for the servant to leave us, then closes the bedroom door herself with a brisk puff of icy wind.

She's just as beautiful as she was in the great hall, but now that I'm closer, I can see details. What should be the whites of her eyes are a deep shade of navy blue, and her irises are pale glowing rings around a dead black pupil. Fine white lines spiderweb across parts of her face, neck, and arms—threadlike cracks branching through her flesh. She looks brittle. As if she's slowly cracking apart.

She surveys me coolly. "That was quite the show."

I shrug, trying to appear casual. "I'm good at sex."

She gives me a sharp, rebuking look. "Don't try to deceive me, girl. I know all the tricks in my realm and yours. You still have your memories, that much is obvious. I don't even have to check your eyes."

No point in denying it. "Yes. And?"

"And the question is, what shall I do with you now? Passing through the barrier I've placed around this region should have wiped your mind of all memories, except certain basic knowledge, of course. But the barrier only rendered you unconscious for a while."

"Maybe because I'm human?"

"That's the most likely explanation. We have two other humans here, and the memory magic worked on one but not the other. I was easily able to wipe the second human's mind with a more potent, targeted application of the same spell. I could do the same to you."

"But you're inclined not to."

"Very good." The Banríon deigns to give me an approving nod. "You're clever, for a human. You're mated to my Favorite, yes?"

"I am."

"Most interesting." She taps her chin with an ice-clawed finger. "A royal of the Court of Delight, mated to a human. I know the memory spell worked on him—I've had him in my presence since last night, and I've done several tests. I had to be sure he'd forgotten his magic, you see. I needed to know that he would be... submissive."

Submissive? Does that mean she... What did she do to him?

The rage shocks me with its boiling force. I lunge for a nearby wardrobe, break a large icicle off it, and spring toward her, the sharp point aimed like a dagger.

The Banríon twitches her finger and causes ice to whirl up from the floor, sheathing my legs and solidifying, locking me in place. Snowflakes swirl around my wrists, too, forming cold white cuffs and chains that anchor themselves to the walls.

"If you took advantage of him," I hiss, "I will *kill* you."

"Calm yourself, girl. I did nothing of the kind with him. I do not force anyone in Griem Dorcha to perform for me, or to pleasure me. I request their participation in my little games and orgies, and they agree because they are Fae, and the Fae love sex. But they can always say no. And they are each allowed to choose their partners. Unlike some of the Unseelie, I encourage consent."

"You steal memories, and memories inform consent," I grit out.

"True, I suppose." She rises and walks toward me, the frosted lavender flowers of her gown sparkling as she moves. "But memories are like these chains." She touches the icy links of my bonds. "They can hamper the liberation of our true selves. I do not alter personalities, but I remove the learned inhibitions, the past constraints, all the obstacles to the intrinsic self, the purest form of the spirit."

"Lir wasn't acting like himself," I say.

"Ah, but he was. The only thing I introduce into the minds of my guests is a poem of sorts, a mantra to encourage loyalty and contentment. But everything Lirannon did tonight came from his own mind, his own urges and cravings. I would guess he has fantasized many times about fucking you in front of his court, and he simply didn't tell you about it. My spell freed him to act out his desire."

My face flushes hotter. But I'm concerned about her mention of the "little poem," the mantra to encourage loyalty. It doesn't sound like free will to me, but I don't think too much argument is wise in this case. I can almost feel Clara's hand on my shoulder, warning me to restrain myself, not to be too bold in my resistance. Not yet.

"You enjoy liberty from inhibitions, do you not?" asks the Banríon. "You have always sought freedom from laws and constraints."

Her comment catches me off guard. "How do you know this about me?"

"The way you move. The way you fuck." She pauses her slow steps, eyeing me with an amused expression. "It unnerves you that I'm right. Do not fear. I cannot see into your heart or your mind. But I have lived for twelve centuries. And despite my best efforts, I have grown wise."

"If you're wise, why do this?" I ask. "Why take over Griem Dorcha? You had to know someone important would come here eventually—someone who would be missed. It might take a while for our people to realize something has happened to Lir and me, but they *will* notice. You'll be found out, and you'll be stopped."

"Anyone who passes the barrier loses their memories and joins my court," says the Banríon, seemingly unconcerned. "And yes, eventually someone will realize what is happening and figure out how to protect themselves against the spell. Or they will find a way to disarm it. Then they will come for me, and they'll end me. I'm well aware that my days are numbered."

"Then why risk all this? Lir was going to review the cases of the prisoners here and decide which ones could return to the Unseelie Kingdom. Why ruin your chances of a pardon?"

"A pardon?" She laughs, dry and cold. "There is no such thing as a *pardon*. Not for someone like me, with the power of ice and of memory. I was always going to be one of the perpetual captives here, until I Faded away. Which will occur all too soon."

"How do you know?" But even as I say it, my eyes flicker over the delicate lines on her skin.

She nods, noting my expression. "We may not age like humans, but there are outward signs, even among the Fae, when a long life is drawing to its close. Our skin shows the marks, and our spirits begin to feel thin, fragile, restless. For many of us, the end is heralded by one last surge of power. We call it the Flaring. I'm in mine now. I wasn't going to waste it sitting in a cell. I intend to have a few final indulgences before I Fade."

"Hence the 'pets' and the 'playtime,'" I comment dryly.

Her exquisite features tighten, growing sharper somehow. "As the mate of the Seelie King, you understand how important sex is for the Fae, how it fuels our lifespans and our magic. So it may surprise you to know that I have not experienced sexual pleasure in a very long time, since long before the Fae-Hunter Drosselmeyer captured me. Therefore, since I cannot experience sex the same way I used to, I must absorb the energy from others. That is why I watch my pets play together. It is like inhaling the fragrant smoke from someone else's lips after they take a pull from a pipe. You don't receive the full benefit, but it's better than nothing."

I can't imagine not being able to orgasm. I play with myself at least once a day, more often if Lir is too busy to fuck me. Losing that pleasure would be a wretched disappointment, and in spite of myself, I feel a flicker of pity over what she has lost.

"Why not use magic to make yourself come?" I ask. "I know a Fae who makes these incredible candies—"

But she's shaking her head. "I'm aware of such spells. But I overindulged in them during my first few centuries, and now they have no effect on me. My particular line of Fae—House Lomman—is known for developing tolerances over time. That is why the magic-dampening safeguards of this place do not affect me like they do most of the others. I was a prisoner in my mate's castle for more than five hundred years, and over time I grew used to the spells and relics he used to confine me. I finally freed myself, only to be captured, over a century later, by Drosselmeyer." She smiles, grim and mirthless. "I have spent most of my life imprisoned or cursed."

I don't want to pity her. Not after she stole precious memories out of Lir's mind and tried to rob me of mine as well. But I feel a surge of hatred for the men who treated her like this. It angers me that someone as beautiful and powerful as her could still be suppressed by males all her life.

You've gotten off track, Louisa. She's diverting you from the truth. Time to start asking the hard questions.

"So you want sex?" I ask bluntly. "Is that why I'm here? You want me to nibble your nub? I won't deny I'm good at pleasing women, but these days I save my mouth for royal cock."

Her mouth twitches up at the corner. "I rather like you. You're bold. Unafraid."

"Oh, I'm afraid. But I like to distract myself from fear with saucy words and raunchy jokes." I smile broadly at her.

"You're not here to kiss my clit," she says. "If a clever tongue was all it took, I could find more than one skilled lover among the Fae in this place. No, what I need is something else. I had a taste of it, watching you and your bespelled lover, and I would like to probe the matter a bit further."

I smirk when she says "probe." As I told her, when danger is high, I'm more prone to silliness than ever. Humor helps me focus—otherwise I'd drift off in my head and shut down completely.

"As I mentioned, I had a mate once," she continues. "Ours was not so tender a bond as yours seems to be, but ever since then, I have been fascinated with the concept of mated pairs. Your connection to Lirannon interests me. So I would like to make a bargain with you."

Instantly I'm on high alert. Both Lir and Finias have warned Clara and me about bargains countless times. They usually direct their strongest cautions to *me*, as if I'm more likely to jump into a Faerie bargain without thinking. Perhaps they're right. I must be careful, lest I chain myself and Lir into some deadly deal.

"I'm listening."

"I would like to perform a series of tests with the two of you," says the Banríon. "I'd like to examine the strength and the nature of your bond, and determine whether it is based solely on scent, or whether other components are involved. I want to see how deep Lir's devotion to you goes. Whether he'll continue to choose you, despite the barriers I place in his path, or whether he'll be easily redirected to another lover."

"You're going to tempt him to cheat on me. To fuck other people."

"Precisely."

My heart twinges, sore from my own doubts. She's voicing the very questions I've been asking myself for much longer than I want to admit. The uncertainty has been there, ever since the wedding, but Lir's memory loss brought it all to the forefront. "Without his memories, I'm fairly sure it won't take much effort to get him to fuck someone else. Your experiment will be over quickly."

The Banríon smiles a little. "Not necessarily. And there are other aspects of the bond we can test, besides fidelity."

Her idea appeals to the strategist in me, the part that likes to observe patterns and watch how they change with the introduction of unexpected elements.

Careful, Louisa, says Clara's voice in my head. *Careful.*

"You said it was a bargain," I counter. "What do Lir and I get out of it?"

"You'll receive a private room of your own, and a servant or two. Between the tests, I'll ensure that you have the usual comforts—clothing, warmth, food, wine. When I achieve my goals, you'll both be free to go."

"And one of your goals is to have an orgasm."

"To put it bluntly, yes."

"I always prefer plain words to hints and subterfuge."

"Then I will grant you the honor of speaking plainly in your presence," she replies, with a graceful dip of her head. "I am Unseelie, as you know, and I prefer my pleasure well-seasoned with pain. Emotional pain offers the most exquisite flavor. Simply observing the sexual act isn't enough—I need to *feel* something when I watch you fuck. I need to experience the height of your passion, and sense the ache of every lost memory when you look at your mate." Her irises are glowing more vividly white than ever, and her mouth quivers with excitement, with desperate need.

"That's why you plan to leave my memories intact," I say. "So you can watch me suffer as you try to make Lir choose someone else. You want to watch me interact with him, carrying my memories of our past, while he looks at me as if I'm a stranger. You want the tragedy of it all."

"Yes," she breathes. "Yes. That's exactly it."

"And if I say no?"

"Then you will lose your memories as well, and the loss will be permanent for both of you. However, as long as you retain your memories, you have the ability to restore his. I will not tell you how, but once you leave this place, any Fae who has researched memory magic can explain the process."

"And whether I agree to the bargain or not, you'll keep using us as pets?"

"Yes. With your consent, of course—which you'll give eagerly, having no reason to refuse me once those chains of remembrance are gone."

I've already decided what to do, and I think the Banríon knows it. While my sister usually prefers to ponder and dither about decisions, I tend to leap into them, to follow my instincts. So far they've served me well.

"One more thing," the Banríon says. "As part of this bargain, you will need to accept a spell, inked on your skin with blood. The spell will prevent you from communicating with Lir in any way regarding his true rank and title, his powers, or your past history together. I can't have you dropping hints and affecting the tests. You will not be able to tell anyone about your situation, reveal your name or title, ask anyone to help you escape, or discuss your own memories, Lir's memories, or the concept of lost memories, with anyone except me and the Twins."

"The Twins?"

"Two blood-writers who reside in the prison—brother and sister, also former captives of Drosselmeyer. They are my loyal friends, and they will imprint you with the spell, if you agree to the bargain." Her unearthly eyes fix on mine. "Do you agree?"

I'm itching to fly into action and fight my way out of here—but realistically, I know that's not possible. These Fae have either forgotten their magic, or it's being suppressed, or both, but they're still much stronger and faster than I am. Besides which, the Banríon has a huge amount of magic at her disposal, and she could easily recapture me. And even if, by some miracle, I broke out of my icy shackles and managed to escape the prison, I'd have to leave without Lir, which is unthinkable.

The choice is obvious, so I don't waste time. "Yes. I agree."

She smiles wider than ever, showing her teeth for the first time—needle-like teeth, transparent and round like icicles.

Maybe she notices my slight recoil, because her grin slackens. "We'll seal this bargain with blood and a kiss." Her hand waves, releasing me from my icy shackles. "Come here and kiss me."

I've kissed several women in my lifetime. Their lips are much the same as men's—usually a bit softer, and they tend to be less forceful with their tongues. Depends on the woman though. For my part, I'm usually the bold one, taking charge of the moment.

As I walk up to the Banríon, I realize she's short for a Fae. Not much taller than me, in fact.

She sweeps both hands over my shoulders, squeezing lightly, and leans in. Her lavender lips are dry and cold, and I keep mine sealed, even when she laps at the seam of my mouth. Only Lir gets to be inside me.

But I won't deny that the space between my legs is anything but cold or dry. I like sex. Sometimes I feel that I *need* it, as the Fae do, to keep my brain and body functioning at their best. And even though I was just with Lir, I'm not satisfied. I want more.

The Banríon breaks the kiss, takes my hand, and pricks my finger on one of her sharp teeth. After painting her lips with my blood as if she's applying cosmetic color, she licks it off. Next she punctures her own fingertip and dabs her purplish blood on my mouth. When I slide my tongue over my wet lips, the blood tastes rich and sweet.

"Mm," I hum softly, without meaning to.

Her eyes narrow with interest, and she leans in as if she's going to kiss me again, but I pull back.

Instantly her features harden and she spins away. She waves one hand, and a frosty swirl of snowflakes fly out of the room on a brisk breeze. "There, I've sent a message to the Twins. They'll arrive shortly to inscribe the inkblood spell. Then you'll be taken to your room, where you will wait until I summon you again."

Without a backward glance, she leaves the room.

6

LOUISA

Not long after the Banríon's departure, the Twins arrive.

Their features are exactly the same, but one has black skin with a mane of white feathers cloaking her head, nape, and spine, and her brother has white skin and black feathers. Both have line upon line of neat writing along their arms and half their bodies. They wear scarlet wraparound skirts, with nothing to cover their gaunt torsos. As they walk perfectly in tandem, each one flashes a long naked leg through the slit in their wrap skirt.

Their synchronized pace and their black, bird-like eyes unsettle me, but I stand still while they circle me, heads cocked, and inspect me from every angle. Neither of them have snowflakes in their eyes. Their memories are intact.

"I am Fionn," says the girl. "This is my brother, Fintan. The Banríon communicated the spell we must write upon your skin."

"Our spells are typically invisible. Only you will be able to perceive the ink, unless we allow otherwise," says Fintan.

"Very well. What part of me will you write on?"

"Your back, I think," says Fintan.

Nodding, I let the fur robe I'm wearing slip back, off my shoulders, and I seat myself on a stool near the dressing table.

Fintan plucks a raven feather from his own head, wincing slightly as if it was deeply rooted. And it must have been, because a drop of dark blood appears at its sharp tip.

"Sister, the ink," he says.

Fionn holds out her palm, and he cuts an X across it with one of his sharp claws. The blood pools in the hollow of her hand, and he dips the quill in it. "Turn around, pet."

I obey, staring at the decorative fractals of frost on the wall. Within seconds, the quill begins wetly marking letters or symbols on my skin, one after another, in a long line across the width of my back. Another line follows that one, and another, and more.

"Will I have to remember all the rules the Banríon mentioned?" I ask. "Or will I—"

"The spell will curb your speech," says Fionn crisply. "It will ensure that you do not break the bargain."

"What about you?" I ask. "Why didn't she take your memories?"

"We have known her for a long time," replies Fintan. "Since before our imprisonment by Drosselmeyer. And we collaborated with her on the memory spell that surrounds this region. She could not have crafted it alone. We wove the charm together, a circle of ink and ice. Since we are participants in its casting, it cannot affect us."

"So you're content to let her rule and take all the glory?" I ask.

"She has suffered much in life," Fintan replies. "She deserves some glory at its end."

"And when she Fades, the memory spell will dissipate?"

"No," Fionn answers. "The memory loss is permanent, with very rare exceptions."

"What about—" I clear my throat, my eyes suddenly stinging with tears. "What about mated pairs? Is there an exception for them?"

Silence.

Shit, I'd hoped they might let something slip about how I can restore Lir's memory.

The quill continues across my back, scratching a bit before Fintan dips it afresh and writes more wet symbols. They seem to be drying quickly—or perhaps soaking into my skin. There are no mirrors in this room, but the next time I find one, I plan to take a good look at my back.

When the Twins finally finish their work, they turn me over to a servant with the head of a deer. The Fae's white antlers have been sawn off, leaving only pale stubs. His humanlike body is sleek and tawny, and he's naked, like the bull-headed woman I met down below, in the prison. Unlike her, he isn't bloodstained. I wonder what the Fae with the bull's head was up to before she came to get me. Nothing good, I'll bet. The Banríon seems to consider herself a civilized, reasonable sort of person, but this is Faerie, and one can never be sure of the rules, or certain of safety.

Besides, in her mind, being civilized and reasonable includes things like stealing memories and making her "guests" fuck in front of lustful crowds.

I'm given a room in the same wing as the Banríon's quarters, except on an upper level. I think the chamber belonged to a guard. It's a simple space, and to my joy, nothing is coated with ice. I suppose the Banríon didn't bother to decorate every room in the place—only the exterior and the rooms she planned to use. This chamber is also lit by candles instead of the glowing orbs that usually provide illumination in Faerie.

"You'll be given clothing and comforts soon," says the deer-headed Fae. "They're being gathered now."

He has a light, kind voice that reminds me of Finias. Unfortunately I keep accidentally glancing down at his fawn-colored dick, which bobs limply between his legs whenever he walks. If I were him, I think I'd be more comfortable having my sausage and cherries tucked snugly in some undergarments instead of swinging free. But I've never had those parts, so who am I to judge?

"Thank you," I tell him.

He locks me in. I try not to care, try not to remember how my father used to do the same thing, when he thought I was misbehaving. He never realized how many people I was sleeping with, but sometimes he would grow suspicious and lock me in my room for a while, until he deemed I'd grown tamer and more compliant. I hated those long, dull days.

There's a mirror in this room, a plain square of wood and glass on the wall. Not really big enough for me to try and catch a glimpse of my back, covered in inkblood writing. But I stare into the mirror anyway, noting my pale skin and the shadows under my eyes. I smooth my hair into better order, then pinch my cheeks to introduce a little color, for no one's benefit but my own.

Suddenly a ripple passes over the mirror's surface. My own reflection shifts, transforms, becomes a pretty face framed with brown hair. It's a familiar face, and yet the features are more delicate, more symmetrical, more streamlined than ever, and the ears are pointed. Can it be Clara?

My stomach does a slow flip—dread and hope colliding in my gut.

Cautiously I reach out and touch the mirror's surface. Instantly the image clarifies even more.

"Clara?" I venture. "Clara, is that you? Are you all right?"

"I'm fine." She sounds a little breathless. "Are you? You and Lir didn't reply to a message from the palace. It was sent a few days ago."

I try to form words. To explain that Lir and I are in trouble... to ask Clara for help... but I physically *can't*, because of the fucking inkblood spell, so I don't waste more than a few seconds trying. I need to gain whatever information I can and keep this conversation going until I think of a loophole, some way to let Clara know I'm being held captive.

"We didn't receive a message," I tell her. "What was it about?"

"Finias and I wanted to know if Lir has received any intelligence from his spies lately, about what's going on in the Unseelie kingdom. The new queen is destroying her own people, Louisa. She's awful. Eats the hearts of her courtiers and guests, turns them into monsters—"

"That's terrible." It also sounds vaguely familiar. If only I'd listened better... "Lir mentioned something about it a few weeks ago, but he didn't share many details."

"Fin has sources that the Crown might not have access to. I think Lir needs to investigate this more thoroughly."

Lir has lost his memories! I want to scream. *You need to help us.*

Finias is more familiar with spells and curses than Clara is. If he's near Clara, if he sees me, maybe he'll spot something odd about my surroundings, or the robe I'm wearing. Maybe he'll be able to tell something's wrong.

Clara is still speaking. "Lir could just turn into a dragon and fly over the border and—"

"It's not that simple." I cut her off. "Where is Sugarplum?"

Fin leans into view and kisses his fingertips to me. "Your Majesty."

I stare at him, willing him to *see*, to understand. The words I want to say won't come out, so instead I ask, "Finias, why does my sister look like a faerie?"

"Oh, it's just something we're trying," Clara says. Too quickly, too glibly.

"A sex thing?" I ask, peering more closely at the two of them. Where are they, anyway? There's something off about the bits of their clothes I can see.

"Um—sort of," Clara says. "You know how the Fae are."

"Yes, the fucking Fae and their little perversions," I spit out.

Clara looks startled by my tone, and since I can't explain, I smile to reassure her. I smile so widely I'm sure my skin will crack. Perhaps *I* will crack, like the Banríon, and tumble into blood-frozen fragments.

"Are you and Lir all right?" Clara asks.

No. No, we're not... help us, help us, please...

I can't say it. Can't say anything except... "Perfect," I manage through the smile. "We're just perfect."

Fin's eyes narrow. "Can we speak to him? As Clara says, there are things his Royal Majestic Gloriousness should know."

"Oh, he's—" *He's enslaved to a terrible ice queen—* "He's very busy. And he's not here at present. Where are you, Clara? I don't recognize that room."

Now my sister looks both suspicious and guilty. She knows something is off with me, but it seems I'm not the only one with secrets. "We're—we're visiting a friend."

"How nice."

"Indeed," Fin says brightly. "Very nice. And we're all safe and perfectly fine. See you at the palace next week?"

"Oh, I don't know…"

A sound startles me. Something is scratching at my bedroom door—something low down, close to the floor. The scrabbling continues, then deepens. There's a sawing sound, as if serrated claws are trying to scrape through the wood and get to me.

Fuck, what *is* that?

There's no exclamation from Clara or Fin, no sign that they can hear anything except my voice. I swallow hard and turn back to the mirror, struggling to find some way to hint that things have gone all bent and sideways.

"We've encountered some minor delays to our travel plans. Might be a couple of weeks." I can barely think because of the horrible scraping, creaking, splintering sound as claws shred the wood of my bedroom door. "I have to go now. You two take care of each other."

"We will." Clara is frowning, anxious, but I don't have time to say anything else. Some creature is digging its way through that door, trying to reach me, and I need to find a weapon before it gets in.

My sister's face vanishes as I move away from the mirror. I root through the drawers of the dresser, tossing the former occupant's plain, serviceable clothes and personal items onto the floor. What kind of prison guard doesn't keep weapons in his room, especially in Faerie? Or maybe the Banríon had someone collect all the weapons and put them elsewhere. Fuck!

There are *jaws* clamped around the destroyed lower edge of my door now. They're chewing, slavering, snarling.

Fuck, fuck, fuck!

I may be in training as a warrior, but right now I'm a scared human girl. I squeal and leap onto the bed as the jaws and muzzle of the creature push farther under the door. Paws slide in, scrabbling, slashing.

It's neither a dog, nor a cat, nor anything I recognize—but it has oily black fur and it wants to eat me.

Another lunge, and a wriggle… it's almost through the gap. The thing yowls as if it senses triumph, anticipates the sweet taste of my flesh.

Desperately I snatch a framed map off the wall. The wooden frame is far too light to do any real damage, but I'll be damned if I let myself be shredded without even *trying* to fight.

One final lurch, and the beast bursts through the gap it created and flings itself toward me, its foaming jaws open.

I scream and smack it with the map, which crumples and cracks immediately. Shrieking, I leap off the bed.

The monster goes muzzle-first into the pillows, tears into them with claws and teeth before it seems to realize there are no chunks of slick warm flesh in its mouth. It pauses, spitting feathers, then bunches up its hindquarters with a howl and prepares to spring at me again.

At that moment the door bursts open, and a fluffy shape darts between me and the monster. Pale-green feathers whisk across my face—two large wings branching from the spine of a Fae male with coppery skin. He's holding a net, and as the thing leaps, he folds the net around it, cinching the cords tight.

The monster whimpers and goes still, drooling and panting.

"Nearly got you, didn't he?" The Faerie who intercepted the attack turns around. He has a large, square jaw and brown eyes. His hair is the same foamy sea-green as his wings, and it's cropped close to his skull. His body is thicker than most of the Fae males I've seen, with more flesh layered over the muscle, particularly around his belly. Two of his lower teeth are unusually long and sharp, and they overlap his upper lip, like a pair of small tusks. It's oddly attractive.

He looks down at the bits of broken frame in my hands, shreds of map still clinging to them. Then he gives me a huge grin.

"Humans," he says, but his tone isn't disdainful. It's warm with amusement, almost affectionate. "So fierce. So desperate to live. Look at you, Rosebud, you've had a scare. Come here." And he opens his arms.

Gods help me, I almost walk into them. He looks so big and warm and comforting.

But he's Fae. I can't trust him.

I drop the pieces of the map and retreat, my back to the wall, eyeing him. Godstars, those are huge wings. I can see the massive arched bones of them, cloaked thickly with fluffy pale-green feathers. The golden tone of his skin contrasts with the ivory pants he's wearing. He's barefoot, and his toenails curve into sharp talons like the claws of a hawk.

"You're wise to be cautious." He nods approvingly. Then he bends, picks up the netted monster, and tosses it over one shoulder like it weighs nothing. I can't help wondering how easily this male could throw me around.

"What is that creature?" I ask him.

He shrugs. "I don't know what it's called. It lives in the lowest level of this fortress with many others of its kind. Usually they are shut in, prevented from coming above ground, but this one must have escaped. I'll see that it's confined."

"But why keep such things here?"

He frowns, and his eyes glaze over for a second, as if he's trying to remember something. Then he shrugs his big shoulders again. "Fuck if I know."

He turns, tromps toward the door.

"Wait." I step forward. "Am I supposed to stay in this room, with this broken door? Something else could come slithering under it."

"Slithering?" He snorts a laugh.

"Yes, slithering. I don't know what else might live here."

"Go to sleep, Rosebud."

"I don't even know what time it is, and I haven't seen any windows or clocks, not so much as an hourglass."

"Trust me, it's time to sleep. We all sleep when we can, without much care for the passage of time outside. The Banríon calls us when she pleases, and we answer."

"I can't sleep with that gap under the door."

"I sympathize, but I am not authorized to give you another room." He heads out and closes the broken door behind him. He must have broken the lock to get in, because there's no sound of a key.

Once I hear his footsteps retreating, I go to the door and test the handle. It opens easily.

Normal locks aren't common in Faerie. Since most Fae can handle a simple lock and key easily with magic, Fae locks are usually spelled or reinforced somehow. Their keys are often made of bone, soaked in blood and etched with ancient runes. But here, in a place where magic is suppressed, I suppose different locks would have to be used. This one must have been a weaker sort, a nominal discouragement for anyone tempted to enter the room and pilfer its owner's belongings.

I glance up and down the hall. No one in sight, but there's no use roaming the place. I made a bargain that binds me here— a deal to preserve my memories, and possibly Lir's. I can't break it.

Now that I'm not in imminent danger, I realize that I'm starving. My stomach feels like it's going to devour itself. The Banríon promised me comfort, but so far there's been precious little of that. I've been mysteriously contacted by my sister and nearly killed by a ravenous monster. Neither were comforting experiences.

If I had any idea which way the kitchens might be, I'd go find food on my own. As it is, I return to my room, close the door, and climb onto the bed, eyeing the big gap that shows a generous swath of the hallway floor.

I'm still dressed in the fur robe, and I have the warming bracelet, so I don't crawl under the covers on the bed. Doing so would make me feel too vulnerable, too complacent. Reluctantly I lay my cheek against the pillow. The big green-winged fellow had a point. Might as well sleep when I can.

Except my brain won't allow it. My thoughts circle each other like a pack of dogs, racing round and round in pursuit of their tails.

Some time later, heavy footsteps tread the corridor. Then a large bulk settles against my door, blocking the gap under it. By the light of the candles, I see a coppery strip of lower back and an ass covered in ivory fabric, flanked by foamy green feathers.

The Fae who saved me came back, and he's sitting in front of my door, guarding it. Keeping anything from getting in.

I want to thank him, but the Fae, especially the Unseelie, are uncomfortable with that sort of gratitude. Instead, they prefer to have the favor repaid.

As I drift into uneasy sleep, I wonder what sort of favor this male will expect in turn for his protection.

7

LIR

"Are you ready, my Favorite?"

I bow to the Banríon. "Always, my Lady."

"And you understand your role at this feast?"

"I am to select a companion to sit with me and share the meal."

She nods. "Take your time selecting one. You'll notice that some of those who are pets today were watchers in the crowd last night. Once you've made your choice, the other dinner guests will select their own partners from among the pets you did not choose."

"I understand."

She pats my face. "I'll go ahead, and you will follow in a few moments. One last thing. Smell this."

She holds out a small ceramic dish, no larger than her palm, filled with a translucent blue paste. I lean close and sniff.

"Deeper," she says. "Let the aroma fill your senses."

I obey, sucking in the sharp odor of the paste through my nose. The fumes burn along my nostrils, and the scorching sensation travels higher, into my head, then trickles down the back of my throat. "What is that substance?"

"Nothing to concern yourself with."

Confused, I watch her glide from the room. Beautiful as she is, I do not feel the same pull toward her that I felt last night for... for someone... I can't remember much about last night. I know I fucked a female, and that I experienced the keenest pleasure... but I can't recall anything about my partner. Not her face, her figure, her voice, or her scent.

My nose is still burning inside, so sharply that my eyes water, but I must obey the Lady, so I leave the room by the door she used.

The hallway is lined with elegantly-clad pets waiting to be chosen. I examine each of them, taking my time as the Lady said.

My natural instinct is to inhale, to catch the scent of each candidate, but I can't seem to distinguish anyone's fragrance. The discomfort in my nose is abating, but my sense of smell hasn't returned. It's strange, being without it, like I'm a cat without its tail, off balance. Even as I look into the faces of the pets and notice their beautiful bodies, I feel anxious, unnerved.

Until my eyes cross a round, rosy face with a plump mouth and two beautiful blue eyes.

I hesitate midstep, and then I halt, looking full into that face. Instantly I feel calmer, more balanced. I can breathe easier. Those eyes burn steadily, brightly blue. There's surprise in them, and triumph, and sadness, and fear, and desire… and despite all the emotions, those eyes soothe me and fascinate me.

My gaze travels down to the pet's body. She's a young female human with a rich, heavy figure and hair the color of sunshine. My cock twitches at the sight of the full, creamy breasts swelling out of her white gown.

"This one," I announce, looking down the hallway to where the Banríon stands at the end of the row of pets.

The Lady looks displeased. I'm not sure what I did wrong.

But she jerks her head in assent and beckons me to bring the girl.

I offer my hand to the pet. "Will you accompany me to dinner?"

Her cheeks redden, and she gives me a glorious smile. "I will."

She takes my hand, and we follow the Banríon together.

"Why did you choose me?" asks the girl quietly as we walk. "Was it because of my scent?"

"No." I duck my head toward her, sniffing. "You don't smell like anything to me."

"What, then? Did you recognize me?"

I frown slightly. "I've never seen you before. I'm new here, and the Lady thinks it best for me to remain in my room when I'm not serving her. So I haven't met many of the guests, and I don't recognize anyone yet."

"You said you're new here." The girl pauses, like she's choosing her words carefully. "New, from what?"

"From… from…" My mind hitches, as if my thoughts have stumbled over an obstacle. "You mean… where was I before?"

"Yes," she breathes, looking up at me eagerly.

"There is no *before*, there is only *now*." The words feel good in my mouth. They feel right, and solid. I repeat them aloud. "There is no before, there is only now. There is no future, there is only the present. There is no pain, only pleasure. There is no purpose except to serve the Banríon."

Those blue eyes are still turned up to mine, but they're less bright now. Almost mournful.

Then she smiles. "I'm looking forward to this feast. I'm fucking *starved*. I hope you're not frightened by a woman who likes to eat."

"Not in the slightest," I reply.

"What about a woman who likes to fuck, heartily and often?"

I glance down at her. "Why should that frighten me?"

"Sometimes it can be—inconvenient."

"Since I have nothing else to do, there is no possible way that could inconvenience me." There's a strange lightness in my heart when I say it, and a gleeful desperation in her eyes when she replies, "Then it seems we are a perfect match."

When we enter the feast hall, I have a vague remembrance of it. In this room, I played before the Banríon last night, with the partner I can't remember. But the space looks different now. Instead of tiered seats, there is a long table of solid white ice, festooned with frost in place of table linens. Goblets and plates of clear ice adorn the length of the table, and countless chairs are lined up, corresponding to the place settings.

The Banríon's magic is endlessly varied and powerful. Her ice does not melt, unless she wishes it to, and she can control how much or how little it chills the air. Magic is a boon to those who possess it, but few in this place seem to have any.

I wonder…

I lift the fingers of my free hand and reach for something inside myself. I'm not sure exactly what I'm looking for, and perhaps that's why I don't find it.

There is no purpose except to serve the Banríon.

"You'll sit with me, near my Lady," I tell the golden-haired pet.

"Do you know her name?"

"She is the Banríon."

"Yes, but surely she has a name. And so do you."

"The only name I have is Favorite, or Raven." I pull out a chair for her.

She seems about to say more, but the Banríon gives her a sharp look, and she quiets.

My seat is at the Banríon's right hand, and the lovely pet sits on my right. The other guests fill in the remaining seats along the table. A male Fae with coppery-gold skin and fluffy pale-green wings settles in on the other side of the girl I chose.

"You again," she says to him, sounding surprised and pleased.

"Rosebud." He nudges her arm with his. The familiarity of the gesture makes me uncomfortable.

"And what shall I call you?" she asks. "No one seems to have names around here."

"Call me anything you like, anytime." He gives her a wink.

"I've thought of a few options. You may pick one. Hunt, because you captured that monster—Cloud, because your wings look so fluffy—or Raptor, because of the talons."

"I'll take Raptor," he says. "But if you ever want to call me 'darling' I won't mind."

Heat rises in my face. The way he's speaking to her displeases me, because I chose her to be *my* companion, and yet he has captured her attention. Clearly they know each other. They've given each other *names*.

"What would you call me?" I ask suddenly.

The golden-haired pet turns, and there's a sly, triumphant smile on her face, as if she got something she wanted. But before she can speak, Raptor says, "I have a few names for him. Prince Pompous. Lord Stiff-Lip. Sir Stick-in-Ass."

"Prince Pompous," repeats the girl. "I rather like that one. Maybe I'll call you 'Prince.'" She says it tentatively, as if she's testing the word.

"And you are Rosebud," I repeat.

"That's right." She leans closer, lowering her voice. "Because my pussy looks like rose petals, and my clit is the bud."

My dick stiffens, pushing against the confines of my pants. I have no response, which is just as well, because at that moment four servants appear, carrying an enormous platter. They set it down on the table not far from us.

On the platter lies a human female, her skin brown and crackling like a perfectly roasted pig. A fat plum is wedged between her gaping jaws, and her eye sockets have been stuffed with cherries. Between her breasts and along the center of her stomach lie sprigs of herbs, and steaming root vegetables cluster around her hips and shoulders.

I can't smell a thing, but the other Fae at the table seem deeply affected by the aroma. They lean forward, their eyes glittering with interest.

Rosebud takes one look, then whips back around toward me with a choking sound. She grips my arm and presses her face to my shoulder. "Oh gods," she whispers. "Oh shit. And I was so hungry."

The Banríon rises, lifting her hands. "This pet was not of much use in life, but now she will sustain all of us. For her body we are grateful."

"For her body we are grateful," repeat the other Fae.

One of the servants steps in and begins to carve slices out of the woman's breast.

Rosebud is still cringing against my arm. She makes a small retching noise. My own stomach is churning as well. Dining on human flesh seems horribly wrong, and must seem even worse to the human I chose.

I should protest this. I should question the Banríon, ask why she would do such a terrible thing—

There is no pain, only pleasure.
There is no purpose except to serve the Banríon.

But if the Banríon is *wrong*... I cannot serve her.

Getting the words to form in my mouth is a battle, but I manage to meet the Banríon's eyes and say, "What is the meaning of this cruelty?"

"Cruelty?" She lifts an icy wine glass and sips from it.

"Taking a human life, serving the body here, as if she were an animal?"

"Are humans not animals?" asks the Banríon coolly. "Are they not beneath us? Do we not deserve to be fed? And what if I told you the woman took her own life? Should we then waste this fresh, delicious meat?"

"Humans are not the same as beasts of the field and forest," I protest. "And to dine upon her, in the presence of another human—"

"Your human need not partake." The Banríon waves her hand, indicating the soup tureens, bowls of fruit, and platters of bread and cheese along the table. "There is plenty of other food for her."

"I'm going to be sick," gasps Rosebud. She leaps up from her chair and flees the table, heading out the nearest door.

I half-rise, intending to follow her, but the Banríon snaps, "Stay, Favorite. I require your presence."

No.

There is no purpose except to serve the Banríon.

No, I will go...

There is no purpose except to serve the Banríon.
There is no purpose except to serve the Banríon.
There is—

I fall heavily back into my seat. My mind aches, like a battle wound that's healing.

I refuse the portion of roasted human haunch that's passed to me, but at the Banríon's urging, I manage to eat a little of the other food. The Fae male called Raptor fills a heaping plate, omitting the human meat as well, and then he leaves the table.

"Since your pet abandoned you, you will have to choose another pet for the orgy after the meal," says the Banríon. She's holding a roasted human finger, nibbling off the skin and meat.

"I'm not in much of a romping mood," I grit out.

"You're my Favorite, are you not?"

"Yes."

"And you desire to please me? To serve me?"

"I do, but..."

"Then you'll claim a partner for the orgy. I'll have the servants find a few suitable candidates. Eat, Raven. You'll need your strength."

8

LOUISA

I stagger out of the feast hall and vomit into an icy urn with ice-flowers sprouting from it. Then I stumble farther along the corridor until I can't smell my own sick, and I collapse on the floor against the wall.

The Banríon did this on purpose, of course. She appeared so calm and rational during our conversation in her chamber, but this was a calculated move to show me she can be as vicious as any of the Unseelie. Finias has told me the Unseelie enjoy human flesh as a delicacy, that it boosts their energy and power. But I never dreamed I'd have to witness such a meal.

A tall figure looms over me, and I look up, startled and panicked and hopeful. Lir has always been there with me during our encounters with the Unseelie, and part of me expected him to appear now, to follow me and console me.

But it's the thickset Fae male with the green wings. Raptor. He's holding a glass of red wine and a heaping plate of food.

"You look like you need this." He hands me the wine first. "And then maybe you can stomach this." He sets the plate down on the icy floor, then sits next to it, arranging his big fluffy wings behind him.

I drink the wine without hesitation. I should be more careful about Faerie wine, I suppose, especially in a place like this, but I *need* a drink like I need air. I swallow several gulps without even pausing to enjoy the flavor.

Raptor laughs. "Gods, woman, slow down."

"Will not." I gulp some more. "That 'feast' was fucked up. Does she serve human often?"

"Not often, but it has happened before."

"And do you partake?"

"Fuck, no. I don't dine on creatures of higher thought."

My nails dent the flesh of my palms. "And the Favorite... did he..."

"No. He refused to eat any of it."

Thank the godstars.

With that concern out of the way, another one rises to the forefront of my mind. Raptor is right; I need to eat. I have no idea how many hours it has been since my last meal, but I'm growing weak and shaky.

I swallow more wine and then devour the food on the plate Raptor brought. He watches me, now and then giving me a genial grin.

When I'm done, he says, "I've never seen a human woman who could consume that much food."

The comment annoys me, but I don't think he intends to be rude, so I decide to ignore it. "I'm grateful for the meal."

He rubs that big square jaw of his. "I saved you from that monster, guarded your door while you slept, brought you food. I might want more than your gratitude, Rosebud."

As I expected. The Fae expect their good deeds to be repaid. "And what do you want?" I ask.

But Raptor doesn't get a chance to reply. Two Fae servants are hurrying down the hall toward us.

"You must come with us," they tell me. "By order of the Banríon."

I give Raptor an apologetic shrug as I'm hustled away, and he returns the gesture with a resigned nod.

"Quickly, now," mutters one of the servants. They hurry me down a short flight of stairs, then along a hallway lined with cells. Finally they push me into a long, gloomy room. The Twins are waiting there, and Fintan has a quill ready.

I balk at the sight. "No more conditions will be added to the bargain. That wasn't the deal."

"The deal is whatever the Banríon says it is," snaps Fionn.

"But we're not adding any conditions," says Fintan, with a sharp glance at his sister. "We're writing a temporary illusion spell on your skin. It will fade in a few hours."

"Casting illusions and glamours doesn't require *writing*," I counter.

"It does here. Every part of this prison, except the kitchens and the laundry, is infused with layers of antimagic curses, prohibitive spellwork, and magic-dampening elements," Fintan explains. "The Banríon has developed immunity to such things throughout her life. For us, those wards suppress all our natural Fae powers except our inkblood magic. It's an extremely rare and ancient ability, you see, and this place was not protected against it."

"That's why the Banríon let you keep your memories. So she could use your inkblood magic."

"That, and, as I said, we are friends."

"Why are the kitchens and the laundry not warded?"

"Because most of the Fae hate to cook and clean." Fintan offers me a smirk. "We like to have magic available for the performance of mundane tasks. The Banríon asked us to imbue the servants who work in the kitchens and the laundry with knowledge of basic magic so they can conjure food, cast cleaning spells, and create the orbs that light this place." He points to an orb floating above our heads, near the ceiling. "The orbs are conjured in the kitchens and then guided in here. Because of the magic suppressants in the walls, they don't burn for days like they usually would, but they offer a few hours of light. And we use candles or lamps as well. Very human of us, don't you think?"

Fionn steps forward, offering her bloodied palm to her brother and speaking to me in a tone drenched with dislike. "The Lady suspects your mate is drawn to your body type or your hair color, or perhaps your vulnerable human side, so we'll be eliminating all of that. For the next few hours, your face will remain the same, but your body will be slender and tall. It is a deep glamour, both visual and tactile. You will also have dark hair and pointed ears. With your appearance altered and his sense of smell eliminated, there will be no reason for your mate to single you out. Even now, the Lady is blurring his memory of your face and voice, just as she did after your tryst last night."

I'm too stunned to protest. As I process the information, my fingers twitch and my whole body feels like it's full of bees, buzzing and buzzing, desperate to fly free.

"Stand still," protests Fintan, gripping my arm tighter and renewing his grip on the quill. "I like my lines to be straight."

That glass of wine didn't settle me at all. It softened my horror enough to let me eat, but now I feel wild and unbearably restless.

I'm familiar enough with glamours to know that there are different kinds, as Fionn said. Surface glamours only affect the onlooker's perception, but other glamours go deeper, temporarily altering actual flesh and skin. This one is changing me physically, crafting my form into something entirely new.

As Fintan finishes the glamour spell, one of the servants who escorted me earlier pops in with a few scanty scraps of black lace and ebony silk.

"Your outfit for the orgy," says Fionn.

She and her brother watch me strip off my gown and put on the bits of clothing. Then they lead me to a full-length mirror in the corner of the room.

I barely recognize myself. My features are my own, only more streamlined. Sharper, less round and soft. My neck is slender, and my body looks waifishly thin. Straps of black lace secure the bits of silk covering the triangle between my slim, toned legs. My breasts are much smaller, nipples perked against the black silk that half-conceals them.

My dark-brown hair is tucked behind pointed ears. It's straight and sleek as water, shimmering in the glow of the orb overhead. I look lovely, and Fae, and not at all like myself. Still, as much as I love the natural richness and curves of my real body, I can't deny that the glamour is fun to wear. Like a disguise.

Or it *might* be fun to wear, if I could forget the reason I'm wearing it. The entire purpose of this disguise is to prevent my husband from recognizing me, so he'll fuck someone else. And I've *agreed* to this. I'm yielding to this twisted scheme on the off chance that Lir and I will both make it out of this alive, and that I'll be able to restore his memories.

This is such a fucking mess.

The explosive sex we had last night didn't snap him out of it, and my blood had no effect when I kissed him. I have no idea how to bring his memory back. But if we can escape this place, Finias will know how to help us.

At the servant's insistence, I add dark crystal earrings to my outfit, and then I'm ready. It's not until we reach the room where the orgy's being held that I consider what might happen to *me* when Lir chooses another woman. Will I be expected to fuck someone else as well?

Of course I find other people attractive—-Fionn, Raptor, the Banríon herself—but the thought of actually sleeping with any of them makes me feel hollow and sick. But is that really how *I* feel, or is it part of the Chosen bond? Is it the expectation laid upon me? Is it guilt?

Maybe I should try fucking someone else. This would be the perfect time for such an experiment, since Lir won't notice or remember it anyway. The Banríon will likely erase me from his mind again once this afternoon's activities are over.

"Go on," whispers the servant who escorted me. "You're to go in and mingle with the others."

I hesitate a second longer in the arched entrance of the orgy room. It's a wide, dimly lit space with a low ceiling, one level beneath the hall where we dined. Judging by the ice-covered implements along the walls, it used to be a torture room, and is now adapted for sex. The ice here glows faintly amber, casting a warm light over thick brown furs and blankets. There are stocks and pillories throughout the room, which will doubtless be used for salacious purposes.

Many of the guests from the feast are already present, but a few of the pairs I've noticed have split up and swapped partners with other guests, or welcomed additional people into their group. The guests wear lavish undergarments or nothing at all. Fragrant smoke curls from a hookah or two, and every few seconds there's the gurgle of wine being poured, spilled, or swallowed. Mingled with that sound is a sultry murmur of melody, played by a group of musicians in the corner.

In the dusky, amber glow of the place, with all the naked limbs writhing, antlers gleaming, wings flexing, I'm both tempted and terrified. I walk forward slowly, feeling like a nervous deer. After all, the wolves in this den just finished eating a human like me. Who's to say their appetites were sated? Who's to say I won't end up as the delicacy on a future feast table, once the Banríon is done with me? She could wipe my memory of our bargain, revise the terms, convince me to obey her, plant a mantra in my mind like she did with Lir. I think he recited it to me just before the feast. I can remember one line.

There is no purpose except to serve the Banríon.

A chill runs over my skin as I move farther into the room, passing between fur-draped couches of ice, stepping around clusters of glowing amber icicles. There are a number of unattached folk in the room, and a few of them have gathered around a tall, pale figure with messy black hair.

I'd recognize him anywhere. By his height, the shape of his head, the angle of his sharp ears. I know the way he stands, the slant of his shoulders, the way he puts his weight on his right foot, most of the time. I know the awkward way he runs his hand through his hair. I know every angle of his face, and the lines of his handsome profile.

And I know other things. I know the size and heft of his balls. I know the exact flavor of his precum, and the smell of his skin. I know the shape of every narrow toe on his perfect feet.

But I don't know his favorite song, or what sugarplum flavor he prefers. I haven't had the chance to really explore his dragon form, or to learn all the aspects of his magic. I know he loves to read, though he rarely has the time—and even though I'm not fond of books, I want to peek into his favorites and read a bit of each, just to know him better.

And it strikes me with a pain beyond torture that he doesn't remember his favorite books. Because the Banríon took them away from him.

A seething determination fuels my next steps, carries me through the revelers and right up to the circle of nearly-nude Fae around Lir.

The Twins may have glamoured me to be entirely different, and they may have snatched away his memory of my face and voice, but they never said I couldn't try to seduce him. This body may be a glamour, but for now it's mine, and I'll own it the same way I've owned the one I was born with—like a fucking queen.

I snatch a cherry from a bowl and saunter into the circle. Lir looks my way, his attention drawn by the movement.

Lashes half-lowered, I tuck the cherry between my teeth and close my lips lightly around it, holding its delicate stem with my fingers. Then I let the fruit pop back out of my mouth, wet and shiny.

Holding Lir's gaze, I pinch off the cherry stem, sashay up to him, and press the wet cherry against his lips. He yields, parting his mouth for me, accepting the fruit. His lips are thin, sensual, his green eyes hooded with lust as he surveys my glamoured body.

When I place my hands on his arms and bounce up on tiptoe, he bends down, accepting my kiss. He has already crushed the sweet fruit between his teeth, and he tastes darkly, sweetly decadent. My tongue slips in, finding the cherry pit and scooping it into my own mouth. I turn aside briefly and spit it at one of the Fae girls who's been circling him, and she gives me a look like death.

Lir sinks his hand into my hair at the back of my head and hauls me in for another kiss. His mouth devours mine like he's starving, like I'm the only water in a vast wilderness.

I think I've won, for a moment. But then he lets me go, with a warm smile, and turns to a red-haired Fae woman who is all too eager to crush her breasts against his body.

I've seduced plenty of people, but usually it was done subtly, in secret, and never with this kind of competition. I think back to when I first met Lir, when he hated me so fiercely because he despised humans, because he couldn't believe his attraction to me was real. He didn't want to admit the way my fragrance affected him, the fact that I was his potential Chosen.

I threw myself so shamelessly at him back then. He was handsome and regal, heir to a throne, and I wanted to know I could have him. I was desperate for him to fuck me.

When he mentioned "love" and being "Chosen," I balked at first. I never expected a bond like that. When I pictured marriage, I imagined being wed to some lord or gentleman whom I would cuckold mercilessly out of sheer boredom or out of revenge because I hated that I needed him to access my inheritance.

That was my plan. A bitter, reckless, selfish one, perhaps. But it was mine to control, to enact.

And then, *Lir*. Fucking Lirannon. With his stiff, haughty manner and his pride, and his thoughtfulness, and his sense of responsibility, and his penchant for books and maps and papers and *rules*. Never in my life did I imagine falling for someone like him. Tempting him and conquering him, yes. Certainly not *this*, what I'm feeling now… this helpless, horrible sadness as he pulls the red-haired Fae woman close to his body.

I could demand his attention. Shove them apart, act like a fool, force him to notice me. I did some of that last time, and I don't have the heart to do it again. Maybe I've grown wiser. Or maybe I'm simply older, inside, where it doesn't show. Maybe it's the same thing.

Shameless though I may be at times, I think I have more pride now. I won't push away the other girl and flaunt my body to Lir. But I'm not giving up, either.

So instead of using my body, I'll use my knowledge of him.

Sidling closer, I rise on tiptoe again to get closer to his ear, and I murmur, "I hate you."

It's what he said to me the night he watched me come on my fingers in Fin's house. And I said it to him once, too.

Those words hold a bittersweet meaning for us. And they are the only ones that might make him follow me as I turn my back and walk resolutely away from him.

9

LIR

"I hate you."

The beautiful dark-haired Fae fed me a cherry, kissed me, and whispered those words in my ear.

And then she walked away.

I don't even know her. Why would she hate me?

"Let's go over to one of those pillories," says the redhead in my arms. "You can lock me in. I'll let you do *anything* to me."

But I'm barely listening. There's something about the brown-haired Fae woman, the way she tasted… My sense of smell hasn't returned, so the flavor was muted, but it was darkly sweet like the cherry itself and yet richer, more enticing.

I have to know why she hates me.

Gently I cup the shoulders of the redhead and set her aside. Then I stride after the dark-haired girl.

She has paused by a pillory and she's brushing her fingers along the worn wood, touching the dark stains on its surface.

"Why do you hate me?" I ask. "You don't even know me."

She smiles a little. "You followed me."

"I... yes."

"I knew you would. You pretend you don't care whether you're liked or not, as long as you're doing what's right. But secretly you want everyone to love you and respect you, and you can't stand it when they don't."

Uncertainty twinges through my mind. "I'm the Favorite," I say. "Of course I'm loved and respected."

"You're *desired*," she says. "You are craved because of your proximity to power and influence. It's entirely different from real love and respect."

My mind doesn't have much to draw from to corroborate her statement, but I have a strange sense that she's correct.

I glance back at the group of Fae I just left. A moment ago they were all petting me, either promising me heights of unimaginable pleasure or pouting and pleading to be fucked. Now they're clustered together, whispering and casting baleful glances at the girl I followed.

All around us, couples and trios are sliding off clothes, slipping inside each other or rubbing urgently, skin on skin. Through it all walks the Banríon, dressed in glimmering robes like black ice, drinking in the sights and sounds.

The Lady wishes me to choose at least one partner and couple with them here, in full view of everyone. That is what would please her.

There is no pain, only pleasure.
There is no purpose except to serve the Banríon.

I could go back to the group I abandoned. They would make me forget the unsettling words of the dark-haired girl. Or I could stay here, with the one who said she hates me.

I can't shake the feeling that she understands a part of me that I cannot grasp myself.

My decision made, I move nearer, crowding her against the post of the pillory, trailing my fingers through her hair. I bend a little, so my mouth nearly brushes hers. Her breath hitches, a tiny gasp that thrills my heart. I like how I'm affecting her, how her self-possession falters at the lightest touch of my lips.

My palm settles on her waist, skims the flat contour of her stomach. I vanish my claws, then tease the edge of her underwear for a moment before nudging beneath, sliding the fabric down until I touch her pussy.

A ragged breath escapes her. She shifts her stance, planting her legs wider.

My fingers quest between her pussy lips and find the delicate bit of flesh I'm looking for. I coax it with slow circles, ever-widening, until I feel slippery liquid coating my fingers.

She's gripping my shoulders, legs apart. Not looking at my face, but staring at my bare chest while I tantalize her.

I bring my mouth to her ear. "Will you let me fuck you?" And I sink one finger into her slit.

She quivers. Laces her hands behind my neck and looks me in the eyes. "Why isn't your cock inside me yet?"

Chuckling, I push down the undergarment I'm wearing while she discards hers as well. Her small breasts are still covered with bits of black fabric, but I tug the material down so I can see the tiny, peaked nipples. I have barely a moment to focus on them before thin, silky fingers wrap around my cock, destroying every other thought in my mind.

I groan, leaning into the touch, pumping my hips so my length glides through the tunnel of her hand. Precum beads at my tip, and the girl uses her thumb to polish the head of my cock with the slickness. Then she reaches beneath my length, cupping my balls, squeezing lightly. The sensation is just right.

"You like that." Her tone is confident, satisfied. It wasn't a question—she knows me. Knows my body. Manipulates it as if she has touched me before.

But that's not possible because *there is no before, there is only now.*

There's only *now,* and godsdamn me, I need her *now.*

I pick her up by the waist, propping her spine against the pillory and lifting her just enough so I can tuck the head of my cock inside her entrance. Then I slide her down onto me, filling her up, and she exhales a long, shuddering breath, as if she was waiting to be filled like this.

Her arms slide around my torso, nails carving crescents into my back. "*Break* me," she hisses. "Fuck me till I have no choice but to come for you."

"As you wish."

Gripping her thighs, I pound into her, while her hands sink into my hair, gripping the strands convulsively. She tilts back her head against the post, lips parted, cries of "oh, oh, oh," escaping her mouth with every thrust of mine.

She comes faster than I expected, curling around me in a tight spasm, her limbs locked with the force of the pleasure. She voices a faint scream, yanks on my hair until it hurts. I don't care about the pain.

I'm about to come, but I manage to restrain myself, and I slip out of her. My cock is hot, shining, trembling, but I have something I want to do with this girl before I give myself release.

"Do you trust me as much as you hate me?" I ask.

Her eyes flash open. She's panting, flushed. She unwinds herself from me and nearly falls over at once, because her thighs are so weak from the climax. I steady her with a chuckle.

"I trust you," she answers.

I reach up and lift the top half of the pillory. "Neck and wrists in the holes, then."

"Are you serious?" she gasps. "Well, fuck. I'll do it."

She bends slightly, placing both delicate wrists in the armholes and setting the front of her throat against the neck hole. I close the top half of the pillory, locking her head and hands in place.

I can't see her face now, which is unfortunate, but I have a lovely view of her back, her slim waist, her pretty, plump little ass, and her long legs. When I glance back at the group I left, they're engaged in petting each other, with the exception of the redhead, who's staring jealously at my partner and I. This was the act she wanted me to perform with her.

But I don't feel the slightest guilt. My choice feels right.

I sweep my palm down the dark-haired Fae's back, enjoying her smooth, warm skin. Then I smack one of her ass cheeks lightly. She lets out a tiny gasp, and I love it so much that I smack her other cheek.

I kneel behind her, my face level with her ass. Between the smooth globes is the opening of her pussy, squeezed together by her thighs. The lips of her sex are glazed with her arousal, copiously wet for me. I stroke one finger along the seam, then change the angle of my hand and poke my thumb inside.

"F-f-f-u-u-c-k," she gasps, with a violent shudder.

With my thumb still inside her, I use my fingertips to massage her clit. Now and then I lean in and taste her liquid, savoring it as best I can with my sense of smell still dysfunctional. She tastes like wine, tart and full and delicious, with a heady warmth that weakens my resolve to make this last.

My cock bobs hard, then pulses, a sure sign that if I don't get inside her, I will come all over the floor. And that would be a waste, because I intend to fill that pretty little sex with my cum.

Getting to my feet, I pick up both of her legs. She squeals as she's suspended in the air, her wrists and neck still locked into the pillory while I support the rest of her. I hold her legs wide open and lift her a bit, until I can walk forward and my cock slides right into her hole.

She's helpless, trapped, suspended in air while I grip her legs and soak my length in her heat. I close my eyes, reveling in the slick, sucking warmth of her pussy, the way she tenses around me before relaxing entirely.

It's the trust that is more arousing than anything else.

Every nerve along my cock is intensely alive, painfully sensitive, but her body is gloving me, stroking me. I roll into her, penetrating deep. When I pull back I almost come. But I manage two more thrusts before my balls tighten and I spill everything. My cum pumps steadily into her—and then another burst of ecstasy surges through my cock, triggering an even bigger load.

Bliss strikes me speechless, and I bow over her, breathing hard, while seemingly endless surges of ecstasy flood my body.

I don't want my cock anywhere but inside her, forever. But I'm not sure she came when I did, so I ease myself out of her, set her legs down, and slide beneath her. "Legs apart, sweetheart," I say.

She vents a little choked sob when I call her "sweetheart," but she obeys. Holding the backs of her thighs, I stroke her clit with my tongue, manipulate it with my lips, tug at it with my teeth until she comes with a sharp cry. I keep licking her so I can enjoy every last tremor of her orgasm against my tongue.

"That was… that was…" She sags in the pillory, drenched in lust, my cum dripping down her thighs.

I walk around to the front of the pillory and bend down to kiss her with lips that taste like both of us. "That was only the beginning."

10

LOUISA

By the time Lir finishes with me, and I with him, neither of us can stand. We took turns in the pillory, and now we're lying on a couch, legs tangled, tongues interlaced. The mound of my pussy is firmly pressed against his warm, bare cock, so I can tell that with every languid kiss, he's growing harder. Soon he'll be ready for more.

Meanwhile, my thighs are sticky where the cum and arousal are drying on my skin.

I don't want this to end, even though I know my glamour will probably fade soon. Most of the other participants in the orgy have left. They don't share the same connection that Lir and I do.

"I'm going to call you 'Raven,' like *she* does, just for now," I whisper to him, tracing the straight line of his nose with my finger. "One day I will call you something else, I promise." It's the closest I can get to swearing that I'll save him. To letting him know that I'm here, I'm going to get both of us home. I haven't forgotten.

He gives me a pleasant smile, but he clearly doesn't understand the deeper meaning behind my words. He takes my mouth again, softly. "Why is kissing you so addictive?"

"I'm good at it."

A rustle of skirts nearby makes me look up. This whole time, I've been dimly aware of everyone else in the room, who watched us with lust or jealousy or both. I've been aware of *her*, too—the Banríon. She kept her distance throughout our tryst, but she's standing behind our sofa now, and a film of ice begins to creep along one of my legs.

"Time to go," she says. "Everyone has had their pleasure, so it is time to clean up, get dressed, and meet in the courtyard for games."

"Games?" Lir arches an eyebrow. His tone is so unenthusiastic that I burst into hysterical laughter, which I muffle against his bare chest. It's strange, lying naked and entangled beneath the cold gaze of the ice Fae who's holding us captive, giggling because I know so much more about him than she does.

Lir isn't fond of games, as a rule. The only ones he'll play with me, occasionally, are those involving large boards, many pieces, and complex strategies. But as they are so complicated and lengthy, and he is so busy, it took us weeks to finish one. He despises card games that involve betting, nor does he care for lawn games. He doesn't see the point of them.

"If I'm going to spend time trying to hit a moving target, or knock something into a hole, I may as well be training with a sword or a bow," he used to grumble, whenever Fin and Clara wanted to play croquet or some such game on the palace lawn with us. "At least *that* would be a useful pastime."

I continue giggling against his chest, and when I look up at him, he gives me a bright smile that cracks my heart right in half.

"I'll play the games, if you'll play with me," he says.

"Not possible," says the Banríon stiffly. "You'll be selecting a new partner for that."

The way his face falls—*gods*. I was laughing just seconds ago, but now I'm close to tears, just from seeing the light drain out of his eyes.

Lir's fingers and legs tighten around me. "Couldn't I have her a little longer?"

"No. Come, girl." The Banríon snaps her fingers at me.

I have no choice but to unwind myself from Lir's warm embrace and go with the two servants who are once again waiting to lead me away.

I look back once, and I see the Twins converging on the couch where Lir reclines. His body has gone limp, and he's looking up at the Banríon while her hand moves in slow circles over his face, guiding a swirl of ice shards. As I watch, several of the shards fly straight into his eyes.

I start to scream, but the two Fae servants clamp their hands over my mouth and drag me out of the room.

She's not blinding him. She can't be. It's only part of the magic, part of the spells and the illusions she's employing for these sadistic tests. She can't be blinding him, she can't, she *can't.*

I should have amended the bargain. Included some wording about Lir's safety and wellbeing. Fuck me, *fuck.*

The Banríon wants our pain and our pleasure. She's sucking it all into herself, filling her consciousness to the brim until she reaches the explosive release she wants. What if it never happens? What if no one ever comes for us? What if it takes her years to Fade?

The servants shove me into a room, hand me a robe, and stand guard until the Banríon blasts into the chamber in a whirl of icy wind.

"Fuck you!" I scream at her the second she enters. "You blinded him!"

"No, idiot girl," she snaps. "His eyes are unharmed. I was driving his memory of this afternoon's pleasures into his subconscious mind, with the—"

She stops short, but she's too late. "With the rest of his memories," I finish, breathlessly. "They're all still in there. Locked away."

"Inaccessible," she says firmly. "He will have only a faint recollection of the orgy, and he will recall nothing distinct about you."

"Fine." I swallow, my fists unclenching. It's a small comfort that Lir chose me, again, even though I looked so different. Granted, I took steps to catch his attention—but he didn't have to choose me. There were several gorgeous Fae in the group he abandoned, yet he followed *me*.

"You cheated," the Banríon says, as if she knows my thoughts. "You tricked him into choosing you."

"I used my personality and my knowledge of him. No one said that was against the rules. You only said I couldn't speak about our history—not that I couldn't use it to my advantage."

"Yes, well..." She clears her throat. "He didn't choose you because of your scent, your hair color, or your body. But you were still a beautiful female, and with the wiles you employed, I'd say his choice was made for him. So that round of our little game proves nothing. The test is void."

I bite back a scathing counterargument and say instead, "What happens next?"

"He'll select a companion for this afternoon's games. And for this, we'll conduct a more thorough test of your Chosen bond. When it comes to sex, Lir clearly prefers women—he has barely looked at any of the beautiful males here. But a Chosen mate is more than a lover—they are a friend. A true partner." The words leak between her stiff lips, and I remember what she said about her mate keeping her captive for five hundred years. But the pain vanishes from her face the next second, and her tone ices over, like a dark lake at midnight. "For this challenge, you will be glamoured as male. Similar features, golden hair, a thick body—but male."

I can hardly believe what I'm hearing. "Male, with a deep voice and a dick?"

"Yes. We shall see if Lir still chooses you as a companion. If he does, we will test whether his interest is merely friendly, or something more."

During a quick bath, I have time to ponder the idea of being a man for a few hours. It's an intriguing concept, and one I've thought about many times, especially when I lived in my father's house, and right after his death. In the human world, particularly in the country where Clara and I lived, being male makes life easier in so many ways. Men are more respected, trusted with more money, given more of a voice and more options in society.

In Faerie, there's still a hint of male dominance, but the balance is much better. Fae of all genders have the freedom to gain power, claim pleasure, and cultivate influence. There's a different kind of inequality here, though. Fae with greater magic or physical strength tend to rise to the top, while the weaker ones with less magic are repressed.

I'm not sure how the Banríon determined which residents of Griem Dorcha would be servants and which would be "guests" or "pets," but it seems unfair that a number of these people have been randomly given the role of working their asses off for everyone else.

After my bath, the two servants assigned to me lay out the clothes I'm supposed to wear after I'm glamoured. I wait, wrapped in a robe, until the Twins come to write the glamour onto my skin.

Fintan writes on my thigh this time—small, neat symbols, runes from the ancient language of Faerie. Today most Fae speak the common tongue we use in the human realm. The two realms are reflections of each other, two sides of a coin. Different, yet sharing many similar elements. It's the only reason Clara and I were able to adapt so well. Still, I sometimes wonder if our very brains have altered since we came here. They must have, because when we first arrived, the vivid color and exquisite detail of Faerie was overwhelming. Lir told us that some humans go mad from seeing the glory of this realm. It takes time for the human mind to adjust, and some never do.

"Please," says Fintan, with forced patience. "Stop jiggling your leg."

"Right." I force myself to be still, but it's painful. Utter stillness feels wrong, uncomfortable. I've always been this way, ever since I can remember. I need something to be *happening*, something interesting, and if nothing interesting is happening my mind creates its own amusement. My brain is always jabbering, babbling, and if I'm not careful I can get lost in my thoughts completely and forget where I am, what I'm doing...

There I go again, wandering off into my own head.

"Be still," begs Fintan.

"Gods, I'm sorry. I'm nervous, I think."

"Understandable. I'm nearly done."

He's the kinder of the Twins. His sister looks extraordinarily unhappy, standing there, holding out her lacerated palm so he can use her blood as ink. I suppose I'd feel just as unhappy if I was treated like an ink pot all the time.

"So the two of you have a unique kind of magic," I begin, and then I wince because *obviously*. What a stupid way to start a conversation. "I mean—I'm wondering just how rare it is. If it was inherited. I know Fae children don't always inherit their gifts—it's dependent on the timing of their birth, right? The way the stars align, the setting, the time of day, even the weather. All of those factors determine their physical traits and their magical abilities..." I cut myself off, noting Fionn's acid stare.

"That's basic knowledge," she says. "Do you expect me to praise you for understanding something so foundational about our kind?"

"No. Just making conversation."

"I hate conversation."

"Perhaps you've been talking to the wrong people." I give her a broad smile. "I'm a fucking delight."

She snorts and turns her face away, but I think I spot the tiniest twitch of a smile.

"So... having your memories must be nice," I persist. "I'm sure you're grateful for that."

"Remembrance can be a curse," replies Fionn.

"Of course. There are things I wish I could forget. Like the first time I let someone put his dick in my ass. I was not ready for that. Should have chosen someone with a smaller cock, if you know what I mean. Or the time I ate red bean stew right before a tryst with the milkman... I farted the whole time. The look on his face... I can laugh about it now, but at the time it was so fucking embarrassing. And smelly."

A choked laugh explodes from Fintan, and then he swears. "I messed up. Let me redo this word, and then we're nearly done."

His sister looks at me, eyebrows raised. "You're fortunate that the things you wish to forget are so mundane and foolish."

My smile slackens. "There are other things I would prefer not to remember."

Like my first time. I was so young the memory is blurred, and I've never told anyone about it. Not even Clara or Lir. Sometimes I pretend to myself that it never happened. It wasn't my *real* first time. It was nothing. Doesn't exist. And yet sometimes it floats back up to the surface of my mind at the most unpredictable moments.

Fionn is watching me keenly. When she speaks again, her voice is gentler. "Human tragedies are different than the ones endured by those who grow up Unseelie. But I imagine they feel no less devastating at times."

I force a light laugh. "Yes, well... I think this experience is going to become my new standard for trauma. Being put through all these tests, so the Banríon can find the root of the Chosen bond and figure out what it takes to damage it. It's like having your heart stepped on, over and over, until it finally breaks."

Fintan blows on the letters he has just written, then looks up at me. "But he keeps choosing you. That must feel good."

"It does, so far. But I'm terrified, every time. Stomach in knots, just waiting for him to pick someone else." I lay my hand on my belly and discover that it has changed. The flesh feels different, a bit more solid. I'm still hefty, but squarer, stronger. As a man, my chest is wide, my arms thick with muscle.

I open the robe and peer between my legs… and sure enough, I have a cock. A short, thick one.

"Well, fuck me." My voice has changed, too. It's deep and rough.

I hurry to the small mirror where I spoke with Clara. There's been no further communication from her, and nothing looks back at me but my own face—my *new* face.

I know damn well I'm beautiful, and that hasn't changed. My face is more roughly-hewn—square-jawed, with a large, straight nose and bold brows. My neck is thick and corded, my shoulders far broader. A short crop of blond curls cover my head, cluster around my human ears, and merge into the golden scruff along my jaw.

"I'm fucking handsome," I tell my reflection.

"You are," says Fionn. Then she clears her throat as if she didn't mean to say that. "The Banríon wanted me to advise you that your mate's sense of smell is still inhibited, so it won't interfere with his decisions. Come on, Fintan, let's go."

She breezes out my bedroom door, which has been more or less repaired, if you can call nailing an extra plank to the bottom a *repair*. Personally I think they could have done better—we are in Faerie after all. But magic is suppressed in this place, so I suppose they did what they could.

"Are you two joining us for the courtyard games?" I ask. "Now that I think of it, I haven't seen you two at the orgies."

"Fionn and I have a different way of taking our pleasure." Fintan doesn't elaborate, and even though I'm curious, I don't ask. I'm not sure I want to know the answer.

When he leaves, I put on my clothes—long socks, a pair of simple black pants, a loose ivory shirt, and a thickly padded doublet. There's no underwear, but the pants are thick and snug enough to hold everything securely. Still, it's incredibly strange to walk around with these lumpy bits between my legs.

I'm tempted to stroke my new dick and see how it feels, but before I can indulge, the servants return and escort me out to the courtyard.

The sun is bright and warm, and I remember with a start that it isn't really winter, and we aren't really living in a land of snow. Beyond the walls of the prison lies the forest—I can see a few treetops peeking over the high wall. I feel a ridiculous impulse to yell for help, but it wouldn't do any good. Anyone within earshot would also be under the Banríon's sway, and even if they weren't, the bargain inked onto my skin prevents me from requesting aid.

The courtyard apparently used to be barren, except for a scraggly tree or two, but the Banríon has transformed it into a garden of icy wonder. She's in the center of it now, hands upraised as she finishes crafting a delicate tree entirely made of ice. Throughout the courtyard, icy trees glitter, frosty hedges glisten, and flowers lift immobile icy petals to the sun.

It's breathtaking. Clara would adore this. And I'm entranced by the sight, even though I wonder faintly, at the back of my mind, how someone so cruel can make something so beautiful.

The mood out here is far different than it was at the feast, or at either of the orgies. It's merry, jovial, energetic. Instead of standing in rows or pairs, the players are mingling, joking, conversing. I'm beginning to recognize some of the Fae from previous gatherings, but I don't see Lir anywhere. The group is smaller than usual... perhaps not everyone cared to participate.

I don't see any of the royal guards, either. I suppose I should be more concerned about their welfare—should have included them in the bargain I made with the Banríon. Clara would have considered them, insisted on seeing them, bartered for their safety. But I wasn't familiar with any of the guards who accompanied us on this trip—I hadn't learned their names yet. It's not that I don't care about their lives, but Lir's and my wellbeing are the priority. A selfish choice, perhaps... but I will overlook the peril of any number of strangers if it means Lir and I can escape this place. Nor will I endanger us both by stretching the Banríon's mercy any further.

Beyond the garden of ice-trees, I glimpse short lanes of sleek, smooth ice, all in a row, with pins made of ice arranged at the far end of each lane. At the near end of every lane, dozens of clear balls of ice are piled into pyramids. Apparently this game is a Fae version of ninepins.

"This is a game of pairs," announces the Banríon, walking back toward the group. "Choose a partner."

Across the courtyard, I notice two Fae pairing off, heading for the lanes. But instead of grabbing snowballs, they each pick up a long stick with a flat, curved end, like a crooked sort of paddle. They stand on opposite sides of the lane, halfway down, while another couple stands at the start of the lane. The couple at the start rolls as many ice-balls as they can grab toward the ninepins, while the opposing team tries to fend off the onslaught with their curved sticks.

"You look confused."

The familiar voice at my side makes my heart jump.

Lir is standing there, arms folded, looking taller and handsomer than ever in a fur-trimmed leather doublet and black boots. The doeskin pants he's wearing look as if they would cup his ass just right. I wish he'd turn around and let me see it.

"Have you ever played?" he asks me.

"No," I reply in my deep male voice. Fuck, this is so much stranger than I thought it would be.

"I haven't either," Lir confides. "I don't think I like games, though I can't seem to recall ever playing one."

"Perhaps it's simply the idea of games," I offer. "Perhaps they feel like a waste of time, when you could be doing something useful."

He nods pensively. "I believe it's something like that."

"In that case, consider this—that entertainment itself can be useful. Fun can be practical, if it diverts your mind. Sometimes the brain needs a different kind of challenge than it usually gets. A new problem to solve, but a problem with low stakes. It's relaxing for the spirit and good for the soul."

Lir throws me a quick smile before returning his gaze to the lanes of ninepins. "Perhaps you can teach me how to benefit from this. Do you have a partner?"

My stomach flips. "No."

"Would you do me the honor?"

It can't be.

It just can't.

He singled me out *again*, immediately. How? Fucking *how*?

Maybe it's my hair color after all, or something about my face, or my eyes. Maybe the orgy was a fluke, and he only fucked me as a dark-haired Fae because I lured him in. Maybe it's because I'm human, and he has some fetish for humans… although when I first met him, he was so prejudiced against humans he could barely stand to touch me… no, that can't be the reason.

I don't understand it.

Lir withdraws a step and bows. "You'd rather find another companion. I understand."

He's moving away. Going to find someone else.

I almost call after him, but I pinch my lips together and refuse to summon him back. I won't interfere. Won't throw myself at him loudly, desperately. I won't beg for his attention. And I won't force his love.

Not this time.

11

LIR

The rejection stings.

I chose the big blond man because he looked kind, and somewhat confused, like I am. I thought we might get along, perhaps become friends. My mind feels so vague sometimes, like a wispy feather being carried back and forth by the eddying breeze. I need something solid to ground me. A companion.

But after I requested his partnership for the game, he paused for so long I understood his answer. A refusal.

I'm not sure why it bothers me so much.

A pretty red-haired Fae waves to me. She looks slightly familiar, so I swerve in her direction and ask her to be my partner instead. She agrees, with a fluttering of her lashes and a pursing of her lips that makes it clear she expects more than an hour's play in the courtyard.

When I look back at the blond man, he's walking up to a Fae male with small tusks and a pair of pale-green wings so huge the feathers drag on the ground when he walks. They begin to converse. Clearly the blond human has chosen the winged Fae as his companion for the game.

What advantage does that other Fae have that I do not? His wings will be of no benefit for this kind of competition.

My partner speaks up, her scarlet smile showing two rows of pointed white teeth. "We need to find another couple to be our opposing team."

A vindictive heat spikes in my chest. "Them." I point to the green-winged Fae and the blond man.

"Oh." My partner eyes them reluctantly. "A human? I suppose…"

"Come." I seize her hand and lead her over to them. "You'll be our opponents," I declare, not giving the blond one a chance to refuse this time.

The blond man smirks at me. "What's your name, handsome?"

"I am the Banríon's Favorite." But there's a twitch in my mind, a confirmation that names are important, and I should have one. Something beyond the word "Favorite." I can't… I can't reach… can't find the one I want, so I use the Banríon's pet name for me. "I am Raven."

"This is Raptor," says the blond man. "And you can call me Louis."

"Louis." I frown. "An odd name. Is it human?"

"Yes." He holds my gaze, still wearing that triumphant smirk. I'm not sure what I did to make him so pleased with himself.

"I want a name too," pouts my companion. "Name me, Raven."

"Um... your name shall be... Scarlet."

She arches a brow. "Just Scarlet?"

"It's as if you put no thought into it at all," mutters Louis with another smirk. He turns away, following Raptor toward an open lane.

Apparently Raptor and Scarlet have both played this game before, so they briefly instruct us on the rules, which are few. This game is laughably simple and pointless. Invented, no doubt, by simple folk with time to waste and nothing useful to do.

"Before we begin, we should drink," says Raptor.

Scarlet claps her hands. "Oh yes! It's much more fun when we drink."

Raptor strides off and returns shortly with a small barrel, which he hoists onto his shoulder. There's a spigot jutting from its side.

"Open your mouth and I will fill it," he says, with a wink at Scarlet.

She laughs and bends smoothly over backward, until her hands and feet are planted on the ground and her body forms a perfect arch. When she opens her mouth, Raptor lowers the barrel and adjusts the spigot so the liquor flows down her throat. She drinks a surprising amount before signaling him to stop.

"Who's next for libations?" Raptor calls, and Louis comes forward. He chooses to kneel and tip back his head to receive his share. As the amber liquid flows from the barrel into his mouth, he cuts a glance over at me.

An image flashes into my mind—me, standing in Raptor's place while Louis kneels before me, only he isn't accepting the flow of liquor over his tongue. My pants are open, my cock is out, and I—

Shit.

I haven't thought of a male that way before. Not that I can remember.

Remember...

Pain skewers my brain, and I gasp, clapping a palm to my forehead.

"Raven?" Scarlet clutches my arm. "Are you all right?"

"A little pain. Nothing more."

There is no pain, only pleasure.

Something is wrong with me. I am not as I should be, I am flawed, I am failing, I am missing something, or I have lost something...

I wince as pain spears through my skull again.

"Your turn, Raven."

When I glance up, Louis's blue eyes are trained on me. His look is both an inquiry and a challenge.

Striding over to Raptor, I seize the barrel and lift it above my head. I flip the spigot, tip my face up, and open my mouth.

The liquor splashes onto my cheek at first, but then I find the right angle and I drink. I drink as if by imbibing enough ale I can escape this game, or perhaps wash away the film of fog over my mind and recall whatever it is that I've lost or misplaced. I drink, and drink, and drink, until the barrel is nearly empty.

When I hand it back, Raptor hefts it. "Well, shit. The Favorite drank most of it."

"There's always more," Scarlet says by way of consolation.

"Is there?" Louis asks. "Where does it come from? The food, the liquor, the supplies? Where does everything come from?"

I look at the others, expecting them to know the answer, but they only shrug.

"I know where the meat comes from," Raptor says. "Hunting parties go out into the woods every so often and come back with game. Or we dine on the disloyal."

Louis pales at that, but he persists. "So there are no carts that bring vegetables and fruit from neighboring farms?"

Raptor frowns slightly, pressing his fingertips to his left temple. "No." His feathers shift, bristling and ruffling.

Louis opens his mouth, probably to ask another question, but a cool voice interrupts. "My friends, why have you not yet begun to play?"

I bow deeply to the Banríon as she enters our circle, looking inquisitively at each of us.

"We were about to begin, my Lady." Scarlet dips into a curtsy. Oddly enough, so does Louis—although he corrects himself almost at once and bows instead. I'm not sure any of the others noticed.

He's an odd one. He stands with his arms folded and his feet planted apart a little too far, a slightly exaggerated pose, as if he's trying to look brash and confident.

"See that you begin immediately," says the Banríon. "I wish for everyone to enjoy themselves."

She glides away, and Louis mutters, "The best way to take the fun out of a pastime is to *order* its participants to have fun."

"Hush now!" Scarlet rebukes him. "The Banríon does not tolerate rebellion or disloyalty. We owe her a great deal, and we must show her respect."

"What do you owe her, exactly?" Louis asks.

A shadow of uncertainty crosses Scarlet's face. "Our existence, I suppose. This place. It's safe and pleasant. We were made to serve the Banríon, to please and glorify her, and we fulfill our purpose daily. That is the most satisfying existence one could hope for."

"Well said," Raptor says heartily. "And now, as our Lady requests, we should begin the game."

Part of me wishes to explore Scarlet's speech more thoroughly. I have the strange sense that she's wrong, but whenever I try to ponder such things too deeply, I either experience that sharp pain in my head or a louder repetition of the ever-present mantra in my mind:

There is no before, there is only now.
There is no future, there is only the present.
There is no pain, only pleasure.
There is no purpose except to serve the Banríon.

So I ignore my unease, and I focus on the game. It feels good to center the Banríon's will, to relinquish my doubts and yield to her request.

Louis and Raptor take up positions flanking the lane. They'll be the defenders, while Scarlet and I try to knock down as many pins as we can. When we run out of ice-balls to roll, our team switches places with theirs to become the defenders. We do this three times, and whoever knocks down the most pins overall wins the game.

It's utterly pathetic. But it's all I have.

"Why the sour face?" calls Louis, grinning at me. "It's just a game of sticks and balls. You have both, so this should be easy for you."

"A weak, obvious joke," I retort. "Are we going to be subjected to your inept wordplay throughout this entire ordeal?"

"Watch how I handle my stick." He twirls it vigorously until it flies out of his hand and hits Raptor on the temple. They both erupt into such hearty laughter that Raptor can barely toss the stick back across the lane. Louis catches it, sets the base of the handle between his legs, and holds the stick at a suggestive angle, bobbing his hips up and down like he's fucking the air. This time Scarlet giggles a little, too.

"Let's see you use that weapon," she yells, scooping up one of the balls.

The balls are made of solid ice, smooth as satin and heavy as rocks. I'm tempted to throw one at Louis, but he's human, and it might do too much damage. So I content myself with hefting the ball, swinging back my arm, and rolling it down the wide lane with all the speed I can manage.

The ball shoots arrow-straight toward the pins, but Louis lunges forward to intercept it. His stick contacts the ball with a loud *crack*, but the stick doesn't break and the ball doesn't shatter—it speeds back toward me. I'm unprepared, and the icy projectile strikes my boot, sending a flare of pain through my toe.

"Fuck," I snarl. Fueled by the discomfort, I begin rolling more balls, as fast as I can, intending to overwhelm my opponents' defenses. They're not allowed to step onto the lane, and Louis's reach isn't quite as long as Raptor's. If I can manage to send a ball straight down the lane but slightly off center, it should hit the pins.

In my haste, one of the balls bounces instead of rolling. It skips right over Raptor's stick and crashes into the pins, knocking down five of them.

"Foul!" cries Raptor. "The ball must stay in contact with the ice at all times or the strike does not count!"

"A stupid fucking rule," I growl.

While he resets the pins, I seethe in silence, half-aware that Scarlet is hanging onto my shoulder, petting my cheek, and stroking my lips with her finger. Louis watches the two of us keenly, and when the game continues, he seems to put extra force into each blow, sending the balls back our way with such vigor one of them leaps up and smacks me in the knee with all the force of a rock from a catapult. I'm fairly sure my kneecap is cracked, and though it will heal quickly, the agony is the worst pain I can remember.

Remember... remember...

"Foul!" I grit out, bending over and cupping my knee.

"It's only a foul if the ball leaves the ice when it's coming in our direction," Raptor says.

"How is that fair?" I snap. "We're supposed to attack the pins *and* defend ourselves against flying balls?"

"A warrior should be able to do both," says Louis.

"I'm not a warrior." But my voice falters as my mind ripples with the shadow of something I can't quite touch.

Raptor is frowning too. He ruffles his wings and rolls his shoulders as if he feels unsettled. I lean down, collect another ball, and hurl it along the lane. When Louis smashes it back in my direction, I catch it neatly. Easily.

Scarlet crows her approval and rolls two balls down the lane. Louis is too busy looking at me, a smile of approval on his face, and the balls skate right past him, tumbling half a dozen pins. Immediately Louis's expression changes and he returns to playing more viciously than ever.

Play continues, and when each round is over, a snake-bodied Fae comes over to smooth the icy lane and oversee the switching of the teams from offensive to defensive.

As the final round begins, Scarlet and I are defending, and the scores are tied. Raptor rolls a pair of balls toward me, but as I brandish my stick to intercept them, they suddenly change direction and skim straight into the pins, avoiding my stroke.

I spot the reason—a bump in the ice, a flaw. "Stop the game! We need the ice smoothed again. There's a raised spot, just there."

But Raptor and Louis don't pause, or listen. They keep shooting ice-balls at us, and Scarlet screeches in frustration as one glides past her stick.

"I said, stop!" I shout.

"What if there is a flaw?" Raptor calls back. "Work around it."

"It's a complication, but you should be able to manage it," Louis puts in. "You always do."

Manage it... you always do.

I'm furious. My heart is pounding hot and loud. Blood roars in my ears. I try to predict how the lump in the ice will affect the incoming trajectory of each ball, but I fail more than I succeed, and the opposing team defeats us by a margin of three pins.

The game is over, thank fuck. But it's an insufferable end, because Raptor and Louis are jumping around, hugging each other, bumping chests, laughing and cheering.

Scarlet lays down her stick, crosses the ice lane gracefully, and kisses my cheek. "Never mind. We can have a different kind of fun—one where we both win."

"I'm in no mood for that," I tell her stiffly. I pull away from her and cast aside my own stick with a great deal more force than necessary.

"Will you not congratulate us, Raven?" calls Louis. "Isn't that the proper way to end a match? And you love to do things properly."

I whirl on my heel and stalk up to him, grabbing a fistful of his doublet. "Stop acting like you know me, human."

A taunting delight flares in his blue eyes. "Why does that upset you?"

"Because you *don't* know me. How can you, when I—" I grimace, my fingers tightening. *When I don't know myself.*

"The Banríon does not approve of disagreements or brawling," says Raptor, with an anxious glance around the courtyard, as if he expects her to appear at any moment. "No pain, only pleasure."

"Too fucking bad." I release Louis's doublet and stride away from the group as fast as I can.

I'm so angry I can barely see. That blond male infuriates me to no end. I can't remember ever being so angry with someone.

There is no pain, only pleasure...

I growl under my breath at the mental intrusion of that line. Why do those words echo through my brain every day? And why does Raptor know them too?

No pain, only pleasure. My anger is painful, yet there is a keen sort of satisfaction in it—a bracing pleasure, like cold wind bathing my face, rushing through my hair, clearing the fog of my mind.

In a shadowed corner of the courtyard lies a thicket of ice-trees and snow-bushes. I make for that spot, as if the gloom might cool my temper. Once I forge into the cluster of sculptural trees, I'm shielded from everyone else. I can still hear the jeers, taunts, and merriment of those playing the game, but they can't see me, and I can't see much of them beyond a few spots of color through the gaps in the glittering branches.

Pausing by the courtyard wall, I smack my open hand against it, as if the cold stone is Louis's face. Idiot human. He's more attractive than he has any right to be, with that brash fucking attitude, the golden scruff along his jaw, that cocky grin…

"You're a sore loser," comments a deep voice.

I spin around, and of course it's him. The blond, barrel-chested ass with the huge arms. His blue eyes are like two blazing stars. They are a precise match for the color of the sky.

"Just fucking admit it," he says. "You lost fairly."

I open my mouth to protest, but he snaps, "No excuses. You always make excuses when you don't win. You can never simply *accept it*."

"Accept the loss, and move on?" I shake my head. "I don't think that's who I am."

"So you let it fester." He's striding toward me, the color high in his handsome face. "You make everyone else miserable, including those who worked hard to win."

"There was a flaw in the ice—"

"Stop it!" He practically spits the word. "Stop making excuses."

"Why does *my* anger make you so furious?" I snarl back. "If you had accepted my offer of partnership, we would have lost the match together. Would you have been gracious about it? Wouldn't it upset you to lose like that?"

"I—" He hesitates, guilt in his blue eyes.

"If you'd been on my side, you would have demanded that the problem be rectified. Justice, equity, fairness—that's what I believe in." I claim that truth about myself, cling to it with sudden, desperate certainty.

Louis's gaze softens. "Games aren't always fair, and they're not worth losing your shit over."

"Losing my shit?" I snort derisively. "I was civil enough." Then I lower my voice, enunciating each word, holding my eye-lock with him. "If you want to see me lose—my—shit—I can show you. Right now."

We're nose to nose, my profile nearly grazing his. He's breathing hard—I can feel each tense puff of air against my lips. Then his eyes widen a fraction and he looks down at himself, toward his crotch. "Oh fuck," he breathes. "That feels…"

I follow his glance to the bulge between his legs.

He's hard.

Godstars help me, so am I.

I thought my inclination was toward women, exclusively. But perhaps there is an exception.

I don't stop to ponder this change in myself. I grab his doublet and yank him closer, angling my face so my lips skim over his. In a low voice I murmur, "Would you like to see me lose control?"

His features tense with a flicker of passion—or pain. "More than anything."

Those three words set me free, and I crush his mouth in a bruising kiss.

12

LOUISA

My mind is a whirl of shock, joy, and a little fear as Lir shoves my back against the courtyard wall. He moves in, his long, hard body against my glamoured one. His hips surge, grinding the ridge of his cock against mine beneath our clothes.

I think I might scream, or cry, or burst into hysterical laughter, because this is too fucking strange. It's too much for my overtaxed brain—the idea that I'm being humped by my husband while I'm in male form, and that I might come in a few moments thanks to a glamoured dick.

At the same time it's incredibly gratifying that his attraction to me goes beyond gender, beyond scent, beyond size, beyond race. There's something at the core of me that he wants, that he needs.

Lir seizes my throat. His thumb grazes the scruff of my jaw, like he's fascinated with it—most of the Fae don't have the same kind of body hair that humans do.

Then he kisses me again, rough and raw, dragging my lips with his. His tongue thrusts into my mouth while his hips rock harder against me. He swivels them, and the swirl of friction sends wild thrills along my cock into my belly.

Cautiously I touch him, feeling along his sides—and then I let myself sink fully into this glamour, into this temporary self. I seize his jacket, his shirt—I rip them wide open, buttons scattering as I reveal his lean, pale chest. My hands are thicker than usual, and they look unfamiliar, but I use them well, diving beneath the torn fabric to cup his chest. I follow the curves of his sculpted muscles and skim my thumbs across his beaded nipples.

Lir sways backward long enough for him to unbutton my pants and his. His cheeks are red, his eyes bright, lips parted—he's moving quickly, furiously, as if he doesn't want to think about what he's doing.

The chilly air hits my cock with an unfamiliar sting against the hot, tender skin. But the next second my length is pinned against the hard heat of Lir's dick, and he's circling both cocks with a warm palm, curling his long fingers around us.

It's an unfamiliar sensation, but terrifyingly good. I groan in the voice of a stranger, but it's me, *Lir, it's me*, and he responds with an answering groan that ends in a kiss, even as he keeps caressing both of our cocks.

Kissing him feels different with the stubble along my chin and across my top lip, but I barely care because all the heat, all the energy, all the focus of my mind and body are centered in one place. My cock is the star at the center of the universe, swelling hotter and larger, burning, glowing, pulsing as Lir strokes faster, more frantically.

And then the star bursts. A violent, brilliant climax. I feel it all, the flexion of my length and the eruption of pleasure, the hot cum dripping over the tip, glazing Lir's fingers. He comes immediately afterward, with a choked moan.

I'm still pinned to the wall, sweating and tousled, trying to comprehend a whole galaxy of sensations and emotions at once, but I can't, because *cock*, because *pleasure*. No wonder so many men seem to be guided by their dicks. The pleasure is similar to what I know as a woman, but it's sharper, more short-lived, and it seems to blur all other thoughts and impulses.

When Lir and I please each other with our fingers, the orgasms aren't as long-lasting as they are when he's inside me. Still, even without that added ecstasy, this orgasm was breathtaking.

Despite the changes to my body, my mind is the same, and within a few seconds it's back to its usual frenetic activity, wondering what move I should make next, what I should say, and how the Banríon will react to the results of this "test."

She won't be happy. She wants to watch us fuck, but she also wants me to *hurt*. She craves pain, and I believe she wants to discredit some part of the Chosen bond, to help herself cope with the way her mate treated her. I'm not sure whether she has fully formed her own goals and wishes, or if she's simply wandering through this experiment like I am, seeing what happens.

Either way, I have the feeling she is going to be highly displeased with this result. Lir chose someone else as his partner for the game, but he asked me first, and then he kissed me and pleasured me afterward.

He's kissing me now, more slowly. Less urgently. His kisses are almost tentative, as if he's exploring a novel sensation.

I allow it for a few seconds, and then I shift my body as if to move away. The movement slides my cock against his and it pulses once more, leaking a few drops of cum. With a low gasp I pull myself free, and he lets me go. He holds up his dripping hand, covered in his release and mine, and then he fucking licks it.

I've never seen Lir taste his own cum. It's another thing he wouldn't have done before the memory loss. Although if the Banríon is right, and his inner desires have been unfettered, he must have considered it before.

Awkwardly I stuff my parts back into my trousers and button them again. The point has been proven, and I'd rather not stay in this form any longer. I fit much better in my natural body. It's more *me*. I miss my softness, the shape of my fingers, my breasts, the flow of my hair. I want myself back.

I retreat, eager to go find the Twins or the Banríon and have them change me back early if possible... but Lir looks up from fastening his own pants. Looks at me with an expression of longing and confusion in his eyes.

"Are you running away from me now?" he says quietly.

The words shear through my soul.

Because I have been running from him, in some sense. Mentally, emotionally. I've been doubting us.

"Not running," I tell him. "I'll see you again."

He releases a low, sorrowful laugh. "I wonder. It seems that nothing *stays* in this place, except the Banríon herself. I can't trust my own mind. My recollections of feasts and orgies here are dim at best. I can never remember any faces but hers, or recognize anyone but her. I think maybe if you stay, I can keep this memory, hold you in my mind. But I understand if you need to go."

I *want* to go.

But it strikes me, like a swift slap in the face, how utterly fucking *selfish* I have been, ever since I woke up in that icy cell. I've been entirely consumed by *me*, by my thoughts, my feelings, my suffering, my doubts, my future. I've been self-pitying, self-indulgent, barely considering *him*. What he has lost. What he's enduring. How he's feeling. I've been treating him like a theory I need to test… and sometimes, like a cage to escape.

I have been in cages all my life. My father's house, the one I was born into. Then Drosselmeyer's mansion, where I was kept by the will of men. I told myself that by marrying Lir I wasn't entering another cage—I was leaving one. So why do I still feel trapped?

I think it has less to do with my current predicament, and more to do with… me.

I've been viewing my marriage as something to be escaped, because I'm dissatisfied, because I seek novelty, and Lir has been too busy to provide it. And yes, he bears some fault for that. But I'm realizing now that the real cage isn't my marriage—it's one I carry with me, all the time. One I keep slipping back into, mentally.

My restlessness, my discontent with whatever the state of things may be—it can be helpful. It has aided me in defying harmful repression, but it also makes me question the good kind of boundaries, the helpfulness of structure. Because I bucked against the wrongful chains of my youth, I also forge myself imaginary chains out of things that are actually good for me. I resist them because I need something to fight, to rebel against. I need an enemy, so I create one. It's a pattern I repeat over and over.

I'm good at recognizing patterns. How could I not have seen this in myself? How could I not have realized the truth that seems so obvious now... the truth that leaving one cage doesn't mean I'm forever free? I will have to keep climbing out of my own personal cage of selfishness and discontent for the rest of my life. If I'm not vigilant I'll retreat back into it unconsciously and shut myself in. And then, when I realize it—when I see what I've done to myself—*then* I can stop blaming the ones who love me, and climb out of the cage again.

I've been so fucking selfish. Seeing only my own needs, my own desire for amusement, and failing to recognize that under all the layers of calm and control, Lir needs fun and diversion just as much as I do. He's dying under the weight of his kingdom. And instead of helping him carry it, I've only been doing the parts of queenliness that I enjoy—combat training, parties, gowns, dances, and fine dining.

Lir wants me to have all that. Before we married, he promised I wouldn't be stuck in meetings or bogged down in the difficulties of rulership. He has taken every bit of that weight on himself so I could pursue anything I wanted.

Except the thing I really wanted was *him*. His attention, his time. Enough time for us to really learn each other like we need to, like we haven't had a chance to, because of the way we were thrown together.

That whirlwind of precious, vicious memories—the blood and the curse, the rat-monsters and the perilous ride to the Unending Pool—all that has been wiped from his mind. That's why he's looking at me like this, with a distant ache in his snow-flecked eyes. He knows there's something missing.

He misses *us*.

"I'll stay," I tell him.

But at that moment his eyes flick to someone behind me, and he drops to one knee. "My Lady."

Slowly I turn around.

The Banríon stands behind me, sniffing the air delicately. The Fae can smell arousal—she knows what we did together.

"Follow me, human," she orders, and I have no choice but to obey.

I look back once. Lir has sunk to both knees, his shoulders slumped, his dark head bowed. Alone in a forest of ice.

The Banríon brings me to her chamber and summons the Twins to turn me female again. Apparently Fintan's blood can remove an inkblood spell, but only if his sister traces it carefully in reverse.

I'm glad to be back in my own body. The other one felt uncomfortable. Like I'd been wedged inside the wrong skin.

After sending the Twins away, the Banríon slams her bedroom door with a blast of wind that startles me.

"Enough of this," she declares.

"You're letting us go?" I fake a hopeful smile, even though I know such mercy is too good to be true.

"It's time to go deeper, to the root of the Chosen bond," she says. "So far I have been focused on the surface, the shallow elements of attraction. Clearly his connection to you has nothing to do with appearance or gender, so we must look deeper. Carve our way into the flesh and bone, into the heart and soul. Only there will we find the true roots of the Chosen bond."

I do not like the sound of this at all.

"What do you intend to do?" I ask.

"Danger." She taps ice-frosted claws against her chin. "Real danger, real suffering. Trust forged during terrible moments. That's what truly reveals the meat and blood of a relationship."

I wince. "Couldn't we have another orgy? A feast? Maybe a dance? Perhaps a masquerade ball, and we'll see if he chooses me again—"

She waves away the idea with an elegant hand. "Not enough. No, I see now what I must do. Go and sleep. Rest your human bones. You will need all the strength of your mind and spirit tomorrow."

She smiles at me with those narrow icicle-teeth and waves me away.

But I can't leave without speaking my mind. I take one bold step toward the Banríon. "I want to amend the bargain. To include wording that you can't physically hurt me or him. And..." I hesitate, then forge ahead because I'm determined to be less selfish. "And I want protection for the guards who were with us when we passed through the memory circle."

Her eyes are cold as the void of a winter night. "Two of your guards were fed to the beasts that live on the lowest level of this prison. The rest are serving in the kitchens."

"And will you promise to let them live?"

"No. Ask again, and I'll see to it that they are all delivered to the creatures Below."

Fuck. "About Lir, then. I want your promise that you won't hurt him."

"If I hurt him, he will heal."

"And me?"

"If you perish, my experiments cease. It will be a disappointment, but I will recover." She advances, scraping her pointed nails along the flesh under my chin. "You are disposable. Everyone is. I would keep that in mind, if I were you."

"We have a bargain," I tell her, as firmly as I can manage.

"I never vowed to protect you from all harm, only to let you keep your memories."

"We are your best hope for finding the truth of the Chosen bond, and your best chance of achieving the pleasure you seek."

"Perhaps." The tips of her claws prick deeper.

My heart is pounding, but I need some hint of hope, so I push my luck a little further. "Have you felt anything, watching us? Arousal, desire?"

"That is none of your concern."

"But it is. Our future depends on it. If we aren't giving you the right blend of pain and pleasure, tell me. I'll do better. We can play out other scenarios for you."

"Oh, you will." She chucks my chin. "Off with you, before you irritate me so deeply that I forget myself. I am old, you see, and prone to fits of impatience."

"I have one more question—" I begin as she's turning away.

She whirls back to me and jams the four fingernails of one hand into the soft flesh beneath my chin.

For a second I think she slit my throat. The flare of pain is everywhere, bathing my neck in fire. But then I realize she pierced me at an angle, so her nails drove up into the floor of my mouth, rather than driving straight into my neck. I can breathe, and I don't think my inner throat was pierced.

But the pain is a shock to my whole system. It screams through my brain, and I'm terrified that if I move the wrong way, she'll slice downward and shred my voice-box.

With her claws still stuck deep into my flesh, she walks me slowly backward to the wall. I'm grateful for the extra padding under my chin, but it feels as if her nails are jutting right through the half-circle of my lower jaw into my mouth, like they might poke the underside of my tongue any minute. I freeze against the wall, struggling to maintain a semblance of calm.

"This is what happens when you show someone mercy," hisses the Banríon. "They gobble up that mercy and then they push, and push, and *push* for more." She drives her claws deeper, until I taste blood. I choke out a whimper.

Her beautiful face is next to mine, her chilly breath on my cheek. "Do you realize what I could do to you? To *him*? How dare you ask more of me when I am already being so very *merciful*? Some would say it's foolish of me to keep the King of the Seelie alive, when he holds such power. Only my hold on his memories keeps that power from being unleashed. He would destroy us all."

"He wouldn't," I whisper. "He planned to judge everyone fairly—"

"Fairly?" she scoffs. "I knew his father. A moralistic Fae who thought himself better than everyone else. For the Seelie, truth and justice are viewed through a lens of other ideals—their fabricated standards of education, of behavior, of society, of speech, of ancestry. Even if you meet most of their criteria, if you fall below their standard in *one* of those areas, you are considered unworthy, and subjected to a more stringent version of 'justice.'"

I want to tell her Lir isn't like that, but it hurts too much to speak. Blood is running warm down my neck, to my chest. It's pooling under my tongue, too. Her claws are blades of ice, burning in my flesh.

"Your Chosen's judgment does not matter to me, nor do I care to grant him any more leniency than I've already shown," she says. "Do not speak to me like this again, or I will subject both of you to the most degrading sort of torture I can imagine. And I've had centuries of suffering from which to draw inspiration."

With a sickening lurch, she pulls her claws out of my neck. Then she shoves my chest, knocking me against the wall so hard that my skull hits the ice and my bones ring.

I cup the wounded flesh under my chin, run from the room, and stagger down the hall, taking the first turn I come to. But I can't remember how to get back to my chamber—the servants who usually guide me are nowhere in sight.

My eyes are blurred with tears. Sobs lurch in my chest, threatening to break out, but I swallow each one. I won't break down until I reach my room. At least I have some privacy there. At least—

I slam straight into a broad, solid body.

"Ho there," says a familiar voice.

When I look up, Raptor's friendly eyes are twinkling down at me, twin snowflakes glimmering in his gaze.

His face changes when he sees the blood trickling between my fingers, soaking the neck of my shirt. I'm still wearing the outfit I wore as "Louis," but if he notices that, he doesn't comment on it. He simply picks me up in his strong arms and cradles my shaking body against his warm one.

"Let's get you to your room, Rosebud. You'll be healed in no time."

"I'm human," I say weakly. "I won't heal, not like the Fae do."

"Ah, I'd forgotten how fragile your kind are. Very well then... I'll find some supplies to tend that wound for you. Never fear, you're in good hands."

I know his kindness isn't free. He's Seelie, as far as I can tell, but he's Fae, and even the Seelie are not often generous without expectation of reward. Still, after all the emotional torment, I can't help relaxing against him, and feeling heartbrokenly grateful.

13

LIR

I lie on a bed cloaked in ice, staring at the frost on the ceiling.

The Fae can feel temperature changes, but we do not suffer discomfort from them as humans do, unless those temperatures are violently extreme. While most of this ice-cloaked building is chilly, the cold doesn't bother me unless I'm in my room. The temperature plummets here, an aching, biting, cracked cold that never relents. I've spoken to the Banríon about it, but she has done nothing to correct the situation.

My sense of smell returned shortly after the games in the courtyard, and my nose seems more sensitive than usual. So even though the Banríon enters my chamber in perfect silence, and even though my eyes are still fixed on the ceiling, I know she's here. I can smell her. Frost and black water, purple lilies and ice, blood and ink.

I have no purpose except to serve her. And yet, for the first time, I feel like challenging her. She separated me from the one friend I could have had, the blond male I kissed in the courtyard.

"Where is he?" I ask. "What did you do with him?"

"You act as if I stole something precious from you." She sits on the edge of my bed, her lavender mouth forming a pout. Her fingers brush a stray curl back from my forehead. There is blood on her claws. "I merely needed him to perform a task for me."

"Then I'll see him again?"

"Perhaps." She holds her hand over my face, and slivers of glistening ice emerge from her palm and float in midair, hovering near my eyes. I try to move, but I'm immobilized. Frost has crept along my temples and along my lashes, freezing them in place. I can't even shut my eyes as the slivers of ice dip nearer.

There's an echo in my mind, a faint ripple of recollection. She has done this to me before. But my lips are stiffened with frost, and I cannot scream, or ask her questions.

With a flex of her fingers, she sends the tiny shards of ice straight into my eyes.

There's pain at first. Keen, sharp agony. And then a softening sensation, as if the slivers are melting into my mind, blurring my memories.

I struggle to hold onto Louis's face—blue eyes, square jaw, scruffy blond beard, round human ears...

I will hold onto the memory of... of someone... someone I fucked... his hair was... what color... fuck... and he... or she? I can't...

What was I even trying to remember? Why strain to recall anything when I can relax here, in the presence of my Lady, with her cool hand stroking my forehead?

"Was I asleep?" I ask her.

"For a moment," she replies softly. Her fingers travel along my cheek, then press my lips. "How beautiful you are, my Favorite."

"I live to please you, my Lady."

Her gentle smile is tinged with sadness. "Would you fuck me if I asked you to?"

My whole being flinches at the idea, and I frown. "I do not know."

"I've never asked such a thing of you. But I ask it now. Will you put that pretty cock of yours inside me?"

I stare back at her. "Would that make you happy?"

She hesitates. "It will not bring me the pleasure I seek, but it would prove something."

"Is that a good reason to fuck someone?"

With an exasperated sigh, she rises from the bed. "No Fae needs a *reason* to fuck. You've fucked women in front of me to give me pleasure—how would this be any different?"

My recollection of those occasions is hazy, and I can't recall any details about the women I chose, but I do remember selecting them myself. "I like to have a choice of partners."

"No," she says sharply. "This time you have two choices— fuck me, or not."

I sit up stiffly, my limbs aching with the cold.

"Why do you hesitate?" Her eyes bore into mine. "Am I not beautiful and powerful? Am I not generous? Do you not live to please me?"

"I do, but…"

"But?" She laughs viciously, then sweeps forward, catching my jaw in a savage grip. "I can't reach into your head and *make* you do it. That is not within the scope of my powers. But I don't understand why you won't, when you have no memories holding you back, when you have my sacred mantra written on your skin." She grabs my wrist, turning it over. Confused, I follow her glance, but I see nothing there.

"There is no writing on my skin," I tell her.

She rolls her eyes. "Of course. I forgot you can't see it."

I quirk an eyebrow warily. She's not making sense.

She lets go of my jaw and plunges both hands into my hair, tipping my head back. "Tell me, my pretty Raven, are you afraid of me? Is that why you won't yield? You're terrified that my cunt might freeze off your cock?"

"No," I reply through clenched teeth.

"Then why?"

"You're not…" I struggle to drag my thoughts and impulses together, to consolidate them into words. "It's not right. Something doesn't fit."

"Oh, you'll fit." She bends, cool breath whispering over my face. "You'd fit right in, snug and tight. It's dry down there, but no matter. I'll endure you rubbing inside me until you come. Then I can finally rest, you see. The game will be over, and I'll have won."

Gently I take her hands from my hair. "What game, my Lady?"

"Why, the only game worth playing." Her indigo eyes are mournful, the irises shining a cold and distant white. "The game of being Chosen."

I want to understand her, but I feel as if I'm a builder, trying to construct a castle without any foundation, with only a few stones. My lack of knowledge disturbs and irritates me, but she seems so sad now that I lift her hand to my mouth and place a soft kiss on the backs of her cold fingers.

She inhales a long, shuddering breath. "It hurts, Raven. It hurts to see the end approaching and to know it's all over. To feel that I never really lived, not like I wanted to. So many choices I would reverse now, if I could. So many tragedies I had no control over. So many wrongs I want to avenge. But I can't. And the anticipation of Fading is worse than the end itself."

"You're Fading?" I ask, horrified.

"Fuck," she mutters. "I'm going to have to bury this conversation in your mind. Lie back, Raven, and let me in."

14

LOUISA

Raptor carries me to my room and leaves to fetch bandages. He's gone a long time.

With some difficulty, I remove my shoes and doublet, leaving on the pants and the loose ivory shirt, now dotted with bloodstains.

When he returns, he fills a bowl at the washstand and brings it over to the bed where I'm sitting, holding a wadded-up pillowcase under my bleeding chin.

"One of the Twins told me how to make a paste for your wounds," he says. "It won't heal you instantly, but it will stop the bleeding, and it should make the healing process quicker."

"What's it made of?" I ask, though I'm fairly sure I already know. In Faerie, most healing potions that work on humans include a vital essence from a Fae—a substance like piss, cum, tears, spit, blood, or sweat. Combine three vital essences, and the result is a stronger potion.

"I made it from my spit, piss, and blood," replies Raptor, with an apologetic wince. "But I mixed it with some crushed herbs. It shouldn't be too foul for your human sensibilities."

I would protest, but I'm in too much pain. After all, Lir told me the healing spells Fin makes have Fin's "vital essence" in them, and I've consumed plenty of those. To his credit, Finias excels at crafting uniquely palatable spells in candy form, whereas this hastily concocted paste looks like vomit.

Fuck my life.

I lie back on the bed and tip my chin up, exposing the four puncture wounds to Raptor's view. He wipes the area with a damp cloth first, cleansing some of the blood so he can see where to apply the paste.

I close my eyes, fighting the urge to cry. It's not just the pain—it's the terror I felt when the Banríon attacked me, the realization of how vulnerable Lir and I really are. I knew we were in danger, of course, but the understanding is deeper now. More painful.

Raptor's thick finger smooths paste over one of the wounds. He treats the punctures one at a time, then presses his warm thumb over each to push the paste deeper inside. I try not to think about the ingredients of the paste while he does it.

"Stay still," he tells me. "Rest like that, and let the potion do its work. I'll clean you up."

With my eyes still closed, I focus on breathing, on letting my tension subside. I'm safe, for now. Raptor won't hurt me.

Something squishy and wet passes over my upper chest, my neck. He's cleaning up the rest of the blood.

The cloth sweeps lower, skimming the tops of my breasts. There's blood all over my chest, my shirt—of course he has to wipe that area too.

Then a button of my shirt eases free, followed by another. Cool air breathes against my skin as Raptor lays my shirt wide open. Slowly the wet cloth travels the mounded flesh of my breasts, over my exposed cleavage.

Raptor keeps wiping, soaking the fabric, then nudging it aside until I feel cool air against my nipples. He bathes each one slowly, coaxing them to hardened buds. A tingling heat floods the space between my legs.

I let him do it, for a moment or two, because it feels good, and I'm desperate to feel anything but fear and pain.

But when he leans down and plants a kiss on my right breast, my eyes flash open. "I'm clean enough now," I tell him, pushing his head away and gathering my shirt together over my chest.

His broad face creases with a warm grin. "I can clean other places too." He waggles his tongue suggestively at me.

Lir would never know.

It's a shameful thought, but true.

I'm exhausted. I'm not sure how many days or nights I've been in Griem Dorcha, or if I'll ever be free. I'm not sure my husband will ever remember me. I'm worn thin, wounded, hurting in body and spirit, trapped, threatened… and the way I would usually react to just *one* of those conditions is to find the first available cock to jump on. That's how I survived the torture of living in my father's house, of being constantly told I was too loud, too distractable, too flighty, too careless, too clumsy. I fucked out my feelings. I fucked so I could feel skilled at something. I fucked to soothe my jittery soul and occupy my racing mind. I fucked to be heard, and I fucked to be seen.

It would be so easy to slip into that pattern again, to pull my shirt open wider and give Raptor full access to my breasts. To let him fondle me, strip me, thrust into me. It would be fun, and I would feel better...

Or would I?

No matter how difficult and disappointing some aspects of my marriage with Lir have been, I love my husband. I do. And he keeps choosing me, over and over, despite everything the Banríon has done to him.

So I will do him the honor of remaining loyal, because he deserves it.

And what's more, *I* deserve it. I deserve better than to give myself to anyone who might be a decent distraction for a handful of minutes.

Raptor reaches between my legs, but I move his hand away firmly and say, "I couldn't be more grateful for everything you've done. But I can't let you touch me like that."

He cocks an eyebrow. "Why not?"

"Because someone already owns my heart."

A chuckle bursts from him. "Who said I wanted your heart, Rosebud? I want your tits, your pussy, and that luscious ass. Your mouth, too."

"They all belong to someone else."

"The Favorite?" He snorts. "I watched you two fuck the other night, but I wouldn't say you belong to him. He fucked someone else after the feast, and he fucks the Banríon daily."

I can't explain to Raptor that I was the girl Lir fucked after the feast, or that I'm the man he played games with in the courtyard today. Nor can I explain why I know that Lir isn't fucking the Banríon. She told me she hadn't forced him into anything.

A horrible uncertainty creeps into my mind.

What if he *has* fucked her, and she's putting us both through all these tests, knowing that Lir has already broken my trust?

"How do you know they fuck?" I ask.

"What else is a pretty Favorite good for?"

"So you haven't seen them fuck."

Raptor looks disgruntled. "No."

I inhale, then let out the breath in a long sigh of relief. Lir is safe from that threat, at least. The Banrion wouldn't get any pleasure from fucking him, so she wouldn't bother. She prefers to watch.

"I belong to the Favorite," I tell Raptor simply. "No matter where he is, or what he does. And he belongs to me, too."

Sighing, the big Fae rises from his spot on the edge of my bed. His pale-green feathers bristle, proof of his disappointment. But he's accepting my rejection. I was right—he won't hurt me.

"You're a good friend," I tell him.

He huffs a breath, gives me a wry smile. "I'm not giving up, Rosebud." Bending, he kisses my forehead before leaving me to rest.

When I finally wake again, I'm not sure how much time has passed, but my bladder is about to burst. I run to the small privy adjoining my room, and I barely make it in time.

Afterward I wash the remnant of the paste from beneath my chin and inspect the area in the mirror. Raptor's essence did the trick—the puncture wounds have healed, leaving four tiny scars.

My mouth is horribly dry, my breath stinks, and my lips feel shriveled. I'm still dressed in the crusty bloodstained shirt and black pants. My hair is a tangled mess, and judging by the weakness in my limbs, I suspect I haven't eaten in a couple of days.

I slept for godstars know how long. And they just—left me here. Why didn't the Banríon wake me for the next challenge? Has she Faded? What about Lir? Is he alright?

I lunge out the door of my room. The stone hallway beyond is dimly lit by a couple of pale, flickering orbs.

My body aches from lying in bed so long, but I stumble along, determined to find someone who can give me answers.

Upon rounding a corner into a brighter hallway, I nearly collide with a servant I recognize, one of the two who usually take care of me.

"You're awake!" she says in a tone of surprise. "We thought perhaps you had gone into some kind of human hibernation."

"Humans don't hibernate."

"Ah, well, I suppose you were very tired. The Banríon gave orders that we weren't to disturb you. I've been checking on you every so often. She also said that as soon as you woke up, we must prepare you for the Lúbra."

"The Lúbra?"

"Oh yes. It's a new game the Banríon has created." The servant's smile cracks at the edges. "It's been fascinating. Many have died traversing it. We are much fewer in numbers now."

I clutch her arm desperately. "The Favorite. Is the Favorite still alive? The pale Fae with the black wavy hair, the one who looks like a beautiful, cold prince? The one who is so uptight and honorable it's *maddening* and yet endearing, too?"

The servant stares at me warily. "You mean the one we call Raven? Yes, he is still the Favorite."

I lean against the wall, suddenly dizzy. "Thank the godstars."

"You should eat something," admonishes the servant. Then she sniffs delicately. "And you should bathe. Once you're fed, cleaned, and dressed, I must take you to the Lúbra."

15

LIR

I get to my feet slowly. My head is a muddle of echoing, clashing thoughts, and I press the heel of my hand against my brow as if that could silence them.

Walls of glowing lavender ice surround me on all sides. No, not on all sides, exactly... there's a passage ahead, also made of ice. The ground beneath my feet is white, like hard-packed snow. It creaks beneath my boots as I step forward.

I don't remember putting on these clothes. Black boots, black leather pants, a simple shirt, and a long red coat, embroidered with gold thread.

I don't remember anything. Words, concepts, ideas—those remain in my mind—but I can't recall my name. I know I've seen other beings, other Fae, but I can't recall any of those faces distinctly. I have no idea who I am, or why I'm here. I am utterly alone and nameless in a square of luminescent lavender ice, within walls that rise impossibly high toward a black sky pricked with stars.

A hollow dread clutches my soul, and for a second I consider crouching down, curling up into a knot of misery before the fearful majesty of those titanic walls and that merciless sky.

But some part of me revolts at the idea of such a collapse.

I do not give in. Not easily.

I persist.

It is a truth deeper than memory, a core quality of myself.

Instead of crumpling, I square my shoulders and step forward, heading for the passage ahead. After a few steps, it turns. A few more steps, and the corridor splits into three passages.

Along one passage, the color of the ice deepens to blood-red. Down another, it turns to white. The third has lavender-hued ice extending as far as I can see.

Which path to take?

As I ponder the choice, I hear a soft hiss behind me and glance back. Along the ice slither two white serpents, so pale they're nearly invisible against the snowy floor. They're each as long as my legs, slender as my wrist, with tongues that flicker out daintily to test the cold air.

One of them pauses and rears up to show a scaly white underbelly. It hisses sharply at me, opening its mouth to reveal long, translucent fangs, blood-red in color.

Shit.

The Fae can heal from most injuries, but not certain types of poison. I can't recall this particular species of snake, but the fangs and the hostility do not bode well for me. I need to run.

"Take the left path," says a distant female voice, soft and urgent. I can't tell if it's in my head or drifting out of thin air.

"No, take the right path," counters a second voice, delicate and silvery as a bell.

"Keep going straight," says a third woman's voice, slightly richer and rougher in tone than the others.

"This is the Lúbra," says the soft one. "You will only survive it and reach the end of the maze if you trust me. Turn left."

"Your life depends on you listening to *me*," the silver voice chimes in. "Hear my voice, and no other. I love you, and I will see you through the madness and danger that lies ahead. Go to the right."

"Do you not see the two adders behind you?" snaps the third voice. "Fucking run! Straight ahead!"

I leap into motion, running down the corridor straight in front of me. Soon the path begins to slant downward, the angle growing steeper and steeper until I'm sliding helplessly, speeding down the slope at breathtaking speed. I can see the openings of more passages on either side, but I'm skidding along too fast to reach any of them.

There's darkness ahead—the end of the slope, fast approaching. With a desperate lunge, I sink my claws into the ice to slow my descent, and I barely manage to jerk my body to a stop on the very brink of a dark pit. The path on which I'm lying ends abruptly, plummeting into unfathomable depths.

I hang there, anchored to the slope by my claws. Slowly, carefully, I begin to climb, working my way back up the slanted ice toward the openings I spotted. If I can get into one of those other tunnels, I'll be safe, at least for the moment.

The voices begin to speak again.

"Choose the passage that glows pink," urges the soft voice.

"No, the green path," the silvery voice protests.

"Climb up to the red tunnel," says the third voice.

I scoff at the suggestion. Following the third voice nearly sent me off a cliff to my death. Clearly that voice does not have my best interest at heart.

"The red one, on your right," persists the third voice. "The others lead to death. This path may be painful, but it's the only safe route."

"Nonsense," says the soft voice. "The pink tunnel will take you a shorter, safer way. Please, please, listen to me. I don't want you to die." Her voice trembles.

The silver voice laughs, a musical, tinkling sound. "She's trying to end your life, sweet one. Ignore her, and follow my lead. Take the passage that glows green."

The third voice speaks again. Her tone is warm and rich, with a smoky depth to it. "You think I tried to kill you, but the other paths were dead ends, in the most literal sense. I can see the whole maze, and I promise I will get you out of this, even if it hurts along the way. The red tunnel on the right."

Swearing under my breath, I head for the pink tunnel—and then I change directions and climb for the red one, scrambling into it.

This tunnel is unexpectedly round, as if it was created by some great serpent burrowing into the ice. Like the other passages, it glows, but with a bloody red light that sets my nerves on end.

"Why do you keep listening to the others?" the soft voice asks plaintively. "I can keep you safe. I'm the only one who loves you, even if you don't remember me. Please hear me. Please trust me."

"I can't fucking trust anyone," I mutter. The tunnel ceiling grows lower until I'm crawling along it on hands and knees, then on my belly. The ice has an odd scent to it—like the bitter cold of midnight, but with a faint floral aroma. It's smooth under my palms as I work my way forward.

"You're running out of space," warns the silvery voice. "You'll get stuck. Go back while you still can, or you will—"

The smoky voice cuts her off. "A little farther. Faster, if you can. It's coming after you."

"She's lying," protests the silver voice. "Nothing is coming after you. Go back!"

"You'll be eaten if you go back," says the smoky voice matter-of-factly. "Crawl faster."

I can't turn around well enough to see behind me, not with my shoulders wedged into this cramped tunnel. A sickening fear stabs my gut—the fear that I might be locked into this ice forever, like a worm that ate its way into a poisoned apple and perished inside. Or maybe there is something following me, and once I'm stuck, it will eat my body slowly, gnawing my feet and legs first, and then… fuck.

Quickly I pull myself ahead on my belly, working my way along the tunnel as fast as I can. There's a purple light ahead. I strive harder, anxious to reach it.

Then I'm sliding out of the hole, slithering to the floor in a wide chamber with half a dozen doorways.

"Forget the doors," says the rough female voice. "Climb. Climb up to that hole near the ceiling. Do it now. Quickly."

The silver voice laughs again. "Why scramble up to a hole, when you could walk boldly down a wide hallway like the one straight ahead of you?"

"Stay here a moment," says the soft voice soothingly. "Why hurry on? Give yourself a chance to rest after all that exertion."

"Climb, you fucking idiot," gasps the rich, smoky voice. "Climb, climb *now!*"

139

"Fuck," I growl, and I sink my claws into the ice. I'm not used to climbing straight up walls like this, and it hurts. Feels as if my claws will be torn right from my fingers. Up and up I climb, trying to ignore the pain.

A sound makes my ears twitch—a thumping or hammering noise, almost a galloping rhythm. With a groan, I seize the rim of the hole near the ceiling and pull myself up.

I can hear it more clearly now—the sound of many running feet, accompanied by snarling and screeching.

"Wait a moment," suggests the soft voice. "Wait and see what that noise is. Satisfy your curiosity."

"Don't stop," the rough voice commands. "Follow the tunnel."

"You went the wrong way." The silver voice sounds deeply disappointed. "I can't get you out of here safely if you don't listen to me."

Whatever is running toward the room below, I have no idea if it can climb the walls and pursue me. Best to put some distance between me and this place.

On hands and knees, I crawl along the tunnel, and within moments it grows high enough for me to stand upright. It keeps widening, the walls receding farther from me on either side until I'm walking through a room so huge I can barely see the edges.

Meanwhile the layer of scarlet ice I'm walking on is thinning, and I can see right through it, down into an immense pit crowded with huge, seething, writhing shapes. Tentacles or serpent bodies are coiling in that pit, opening titanic jaws now and then, snapping upward as if they're hoping I'll fall through the ice and tumble into one of their maws.

My steps falter, and as my right boot lands on the thin layer of ice, it starts to give way with an unsettling crunch. Cracks branch from beneath my boot.

"Angle left." It's the voice I've been following—rich and warm, with a trace of sultry hoarseness, a velvety feminine depth.

I swerve left immediately.

"Please," intercedes the soft, silken voice. "Please stop listening to her... she's leading you to certain death. Turn right, if you value your life."

The high, silvery voice chimes in. "No, no, they're both wrong... poor sweet male, beautiful boy, you are going to be lost forever if you don't go back the way you came."

The voices intersect, clamoring over each other until I can barely distinguish words. I can't hear anyone's warnings or directions.

I stop short and bellow, "Enough! Who the fuck are you?"

"Your guide..."

"Your destiny..."

"Wisdom..."

"Safety..."

"I care for you, I want to protect you, I'm your only hope..."

Titles and words echo in the air, coming from all different directions. But the rich, smoky voice speaks, low and distinct, "I'm someone who loves you."

The words vibrate in the center of my chest, along my bones, through my blood. Without really knowing why, I believe her, as surely as I believe in my own existence.

"Guide me then," I say, in a tone just as low and intense as hers. "You've kept me alive this far. I trust you."

"Walk ten paces forward." As she speaks, the voices of the other two fade to a distant babble. "Then turn right. That's it. Now five paces, then a sharp left."

I follow her directions, my body tense with anxiety as the monsters surge and roll far below me. Just a sheet of fragile ice between me and them.

"Quick, now," she says. "Three running steps, then leap as far as you can, straight ahead. And then you're going to have to trust me more than ever. Can you do that?"

My muscles tighten, preparing to follow her instructions. "My life is in your hands."

16

LOUISA

I'm sitting beside the Banríon, atop a tall pillar overlooking the maze she created.

It's more than a maze, really. It's a multilevel obstacle course filled with pitfalls, traps, and monsters, both real and illusory. Moments ago, Lir was nearly cornered and eaten by beasts much like the one that chewed its way into my bedroom. Thank the godstars he listened to me and climbed to the only escape route, the tunnel near the ceiling, right before the swarm of monsters poured out of every corridor into that central room.

If I had to rely on my normal human vision, I wouldn't be able to see his progress from this vantage point. I wouldn't be able to gauge every angle or perceive what lies ahead. But when this test started, the Banríon placed goggles of ice over my eyes, allowing me to see right through the walls of the Lúbra, to perceive depth, distance, and danger. In some places, like the sheet of ice Lir is traversing now, the safe spots have a sparkling sheen to them, one he can't perceive. But I can detect those areas and direct him to safe footing.

I've always been quick to calculate threats and observe patterns. I found the only safe route through the Lúbra within the first couple of minutes—marked out the whole thing in my mind. Since then, my main concern has been getting Lir to listen to *me*, not the other two pets the Banríon enlisted to confuse him. All three of our voices are being magically communicated to him, thanks to inkblood spells written on our skin and his.

The Banríon told me she suppressed all his memories again—only this time she erased his recollection of the entire time he has spent at Griem Dorcha. She said she wanted him "unencumbered" by our recent past, but I know she wants him helpless and vulnerable.

And yet, even with her magic gripping his mind, blotting out everything but the present, he remains strong, steady, clever, and brave. My admiration for him has grown since he first regained consciousness and began to travel through the maze. And when he began to listen to me, even from that very first choice, I couldn't repress a grin of triumph.

He kept obeying my voice, despite the fact that he nearly slid down to his death the first time he heeded my directions. But I knew he'd be able to stop his fall, and descending that slope was the only way to access the escape route.

Even now, as he traverses the perilous sheet of ice, he obeys my every command instantly—a good thing, because he's one wrong step away from plummeting to a death no Fae could survive.

My brain is on high alert, noting the areas of sparkling color that mark the thicker spots in the ice, the safe route. I take in the visual information, process it at lightning speed, communicate it to Lir in terse, crisp phrases. He runs when I say to run, leaps when I tell him to leap.

Once Lir has navigated the sheet of ice, he stands on the brink of a dark chasm. I can perceive the narrow, invisible bridge spanning the emptiness, but since he's hesitating, I suspect he can't.

"Do you see the bridge?" I ask him.

"What bridge?" His voice, communicated to me through the spell, is stiff and strained.

"This is the part I mentioned, where you have to trust me implicitly."

The other two pets are wailing and yammering, trying to get his attention again, but he acts as if he can't hear them. He's choosing to listen to me alone.

"One step to the right," I tell him. "Now move your foot forward. You're going to think you're stepping into thin air, but you aren't. There's a bridge you can't see. It's narrow, barely enough room for you to stand normally. It's not straight, either—it has twists and turns. You have to move slowly and listen to me carefully."

Lir sidesteps, then slides one boot onto the bridge. "Fuck," he murmurs. "You're right. I feel it, but I can't see it."

"Good. Two steps forward, then sharp left."

Little by little, I help him cross the chasm. My palms, my cleavage, and the back of my neck are sweating—I feel drops rolling down my spine, despite the chilly air. A moment ago, I heard the Banríon sigh gustily, and I'm terrified she will lose her patience and decide to introduce another dangerous complication for the benefit of the audience.

Most of the remaining Fae in the prison are watching the show from tiered benches of ice the Banríon created for them.

They're wearing goggles similar to mine so they can observe the dangers awaiting Lir. Every time I've saved him, they've voiced disappointed groans. They're ravenous for blood, eager for him to be torn and devoured.

I'm determined to disappoint them.

Once Lir reaches the other side of the bridge, I guide him through a corridor where icy blocks ram down from the ceiling every few seconds, threatening to crush him flat. My brain quickly catches on to their rhythm, and as I shout terse instructions, Lir follows my guidance so flawlessly that I feel tears gathering in my eyes, tears of wonder at the marvel of *us*. We make a better team than I imagined. We are capable of so much more than we thought.

He's almost out of the maze now, treading a long corridor that leads to a pitch-black cave. I squint, trying to perceive what's in the cave, but even with my goggles, I can't. I only know that beyond that cave lie the doors leading out of the maze.

"Almost there," I assure Lir.

Suddenly, sharp-nailed fingers rip the goggles from my face.

The Banríon looms over me, her eyes hard and bright. "You're part of the final test in the Lúbra. We must prepare you quickly."

She conjures a snowy whirlwind that encircles us both and carries us down from the top of our observation pillar. When we land, I'm gasping from the shock.

The Twins are waiting for us. Fionn holds one of her quills, dripping with her brother's blood. Swiftly she retraces the line of Fintan's communication spell, writing it backwards, cutting me off from speaking with Lir and the other two females.

Fintan doesn't look at me while his sister works, but a muscle along his jaw twitches.

"Fintan," I say. "What's going on?"

He casts me a swift, sorrowful glance, bites his lip, and turns away again.

"Fionn?" I ask.

But she only shakes her head.

The moment the Twins step away, four Fae approach me. Their claws slash through my clothing, peeling it rapidly away from my skin, rendering me naked in seconds. My warming bracelet is removed as well.

"What the fuck?" I gasp, but they don't reply. One of them sprays my body with a hideous, choking perfume. Another grips my head and holds it still while a third Fae approaches, brandishing a large needle and black thread in his gloved hands.

All this time I've been holding back because I've known that my training and strength can't really help me here. But as that needle approaches my lips, I lose all restraint. I jab my elbow into the ribs of the Fae behind me. He's startled, and his grip on my head eases just enough for me to lunge free. I whirl, using my thick, strong legs to advantage in a powerful kick that knocks the needle-wielding Fae off balance. I smash a punch into the delicate jaw of a Fae female, then slam another kick into someone's gut.

Before I can do any more damage, bone-freezing cold slides up my legs and over my arms, locking me in place. "We have no time for this," seethes the Banríon. "Be glad we're only stitching your lips instead of cutting out your tongue."

"If you're trying to take my voice, you could do it with magic," I say.

The Banríon looks me right in the eyes and smiles.

Of course she could silence me with magic. She's choosing not to. She *wants* to hurt me. Blames me, somehow, for the strength of my bond with Lir.

"You cheated," she says. "You told him you love him."

"I didn't break our deal. I said nothing about our past. If you didn't want me to express my current feelings, you should have made that a specific criterion of the bargain. The fact that I was able to say it means it's allowed by the terms of the spell. Besides, one of your other pets claimed to love him, too. Yet he only believed *me*."

She glares at me, her lavender lip hitched to reveal a glint of her icy teeth.

"Every time he chooses me, you hate me more," I say. "But it isn't my fault your mate was cruel to you. It's not my fault your bond was flawed—" My words break off as the Fae with the needle roughly pinches my lips into a pout. He pierces my lower lip at the corner, shoves the needle through my upper lip, then loops back to the lower one. Over and over he stitches with the thick black thread, while blood drips down my lips and chin.

The pain surpasses anything I've ever felt. Worse than the agony of the needle is the anguish of being silenced.

When he's done, I can't move my lips without feeling the horrible tug of the stitches, so I keep them pinned together, as still as possible.

I tell myself I can be healed after this test. If the Banríon won't allow anyone to heal me, then Finias will fix me somehow. I will endure this, survive this, get myself and Lir home to Fin and my sister. I hope to the godstars they're alright.

Clara and I knew what we were getting into when we decided to stay in Faerie. At least, I thought I knew. But I hadn't experienced Unseelie cruelty the way she had. Maybe I was naïve to think I'd already endured the worst parts of my existence in this realm.

The ice melts away from my body, but before I can fight back again, cords are wrapped hastily around my wrists and ankles, binding them together.

"Put her in the cave with the others," says the Banríon.

I'm lifted and carried away while the onlookers roar with eager anticipation.

The Fae handle me carelessly, like I'm a sack of potatoes, so my view is the ground first, then the sky, then a pair of wooden doors—the exit of the maze. They yank open the doors and toss me naked into the darkness beyond. Then they slam the exit shut.

Blackness.

I can't see anything. I may as well have been blindfolded. My nostrils are stinging, coated with that horrible stuff they sprayed on me—something to confuse Lir's sense of smell, if I had to guess.

My senses of touch and hearing remain intact. I'm lying amid nude bodies, also bound and silenced, judging by the brush of smooth skin, the roughness of rope, and the muffled moans all around me. I can tell that the ones nearest me are breathing through their noses, not their mouths. Perhaps their lips were stitched shut as well.

I have no idea what test the Banríon has devised this time. There's nothing sexual about the naked, terrified tangle of panicked bodies lying clumped together in the ink-black cave. This isn't about Lir choosing a lover—this is about something deeper.

It's about my fucking survival.

17

LIR

My guiding voice hasn't spoken in a while, and it unsettles me. She said I was "almost there"—almost out of this death-trap. But I've been walking this corridor for what seems like ages, with no end in sight.

"Are you there?" I call.

Instead of my chosen guide, the silvery voice speaks to me. "You will enter a cave of prisoners. There is a door at the far end. Choose one captive to escape with you. The rest will be fed to the beasts of the maze."

"Where is the one who guided me?" I demand. "I want to hear her speak."

"She cannot speak to you," replies the silvery one. "You can save her, or doom her."

Shock throbs through my heart. "Does that mean she's in the cave? She's a captive?"

No answer.

My mind understands what race I am, knows there is a world beyond this place, and yet I can't remember meeting a single living soul. I can't remember anything but this wretched maze of ice, and the beasts within it. My guide was my only friend. She didn't merely claim to love me—I could hear the truth of it in her voice.

And now I must find her and save her, or she will be consumed by the beasts of the maze.

It shouldn't be difficult to locate her. I simply have to ask the captives to speak. I could distinguish her tones among any number of voices, I'm sure of it.

There's a door ahead—the end of this passage. The cave must lie beyond.

The moment I open the door and step through, it slams behind me with such violent force I'm thrown forward into the thick darkness. My claws squelch into something soft, and I hear a groan.

Fuck.

I vanish my claws quickly and slide my palms over the area where I landed. It's a naked body, long and lean. My fingertips encounter two hands, bound with rope whose fibers sting me. It must be infused with shreds of iron. Feeling along the body, I trace lumps of spine and two gauzy wings trailing from between bare shoulder blades.

"Who are you?" I ask.

The Fae only gives a low groan. It sounds as if something is covering their mouth.

Cautiously I feel upward, along their neck, planning to remove their gag. But instead of fabric, I encounter lips sealed with thick thread in crooked stitches. When I touch those stitches, pain zaps through my fingers, sending shivers of weakness through my body.

"Fuck," I whisper as a suspicion floods my mind.

Sure enough, as I feel around and investigate the nearest bodies by touch, I discover that each one is bound with iron-flecked rope at the wrists and ankles, and that their lips are sewn shut with thread that must be cursed as well as iron-infused.

My frustration grows as I grapple with the fact that I know about curses and iron, and yet I can't recall my fucking *name*.

The air in the cave is close and thick, drenched in a disgusting odor that makes my sensitive nose prickle uncomfortably. I breathe through my mouth as I fumble forward in the dark.

How am I supposed to find the woman who served as my guide? She can't speak to me, and I can't grip the stitches on the captives' mouths long enough to pluck them free—not without weakening myself to the point of death.

Perhaps I should find the exit first, and then decide what to do.

I crawl ahead, pushing against limbs so their owners will move aside. I don't want to crawl over anyone and cause them more pain, especially not when they are likely to be devoured soon.

Somewhere in the depths of my soul there's a tug of grief, of something more than compassion for the doomed prisoners. It's beyond simple pity—it's almost a sense of responsibility. As if it's my duty to preserve their lives, to protect them.

But greater still is the urge to find the owner of that voice. I can recall it clearly—warm and smoky. That unique earthiness, that imperfect roughness… it was more human than Fae. Perhaps I'm looking for a human. A human woman. And there was a rich shape and substance to the voice, a solidity to the sound. A woman, flawed and mortal, but with confidence, boldness. Perhaps thicker of body. A woman with a voice like that, with sultry inflections like those—I'd wager she enjoys pleasure and allows herself indulgences of all kinds.

I nudge aside another body, creating enough space for me to stand upright. But when I rise, my head smacks into rock. Apparently the ceiling of the cave was only high near the entrance, and it's low elsewhere. Mumbling a curse, I sit down instead, while pain rings through my skull.

"I'm looking for the one who guided me through the maze." My voice doesn't carry far through the thick, cloying reek of the cave, but I persist. "If you're the one who kept me safe, come to me. I want to save you."

Moans and scuffling noises intensify in the darkness as the bound bodies move, struggling to reach me. Fuck, that was a foolish thing to say. Now every captive in this cave is going to pretend they're the one I seek so they can escape.

Something drifts toward me, a faint sound mingled with the desperate moans of the prisoners. But this isn't a moan, it's music. Someone is humming.

I could swear I've heard the song before, yet I can't remember where. The melody resonates in a place deeper than memory, and I begin to move toward it.

Bodies thrash in the dark, bumping against me in a mute attempt to capture my attention, but I crawl on, through the nauseating odor and the darkness and the panicked captives, toward the humming.

The closer I get, the better I can distinguish the voice. It's muffled, like the others, and sometimes it falters, but it's rich, melodic, husky—a woman's voice, I think. It could be the voice of my guide.

My fingers close on a foot. It twitches away—ticklish, perhaps. My hand roves over a plump ankle laced with rope, then a rounded calf, a dimpled knee, a thick thigh. The humming vibrates through my palm as my touch traverses a generous belly and the contour of a heavy breast. I keep going, up the neck to the soft cheek, and from there to the rounded ear and silken hair of the singer.

She's still humming, but the sound is fragile now. Something wet and warm trickles over my finger. Tentatively I place the wet finger in my mouth, and salt bursts over my tongue. She's crying.

I cup her face between my hands, my thumbs hovering lightly over the stitches across her mouth. "You're the one, aren't you?" I whisper. "You're my guide."

She nods against my palms. A tiny sob escapes her, and I feel tears gathering in my own eyes.

"This one!" I shout to whoever is listening. "I choose this one!"

There's no response. No doors are flung open, no daylight streams into the cave. But the other captives stir more frantically, as if they sense their last chance of life fading away.

The woman's feet and hands are bound, but the iron infusion isn't as strong in the ropes as it is with the stitches. I'm able to pick the knot at her ankles after a few tries, with a moment's rest now and then to catch my breath and recover from the pain. But the prisoners are closing in—I can hear flesh smacking and surging against flesh, cries of pain as they worm their way over each other to get near us. I'm not sure how they think moving closer will help them escape. Perhaps they simply want to hem us in and prevent us from escaping, since they have no hope for themselves.

I graze my lips along the woman's cheek until I reach her ear. "We have to crawl. Are you with me?"

She nods again.

Together we struggle along on hands and knees, shoving a path through the other captives. They can feel the clothes I'm wearing. They know I'm not one of them. The chorus of wordless groans amplifies in agony and intensity as we go.

I've lost all sense of where I entered the cave, and I'm afraid I'll find a door, only to open it and discover we're back in the maze.

The woman beside me is crawling as best she can with her wrists lashed together. At last she pauses, braces herself against my shoulder, and grips my other arm with her bound hands. She pulls my arm over and shoves my palm against something—hard stone. The wall of the cave.

I want to kiss her. With the cave wall to guide us, we're bound to come to either the entrance or the exit soon.

But before we can move any farther, a beam of light slashes into the darkness. A door has opened, shedding a white glare over the sea of bare, thrashing bodies.

I can see icy walls through the doorway. It's the entrance I came through, the way into the maze.

A flurry of motion erupts by that door, a storm of muffled screaming and vicious snarling. I can hear flesh tearing, teeth scraping on bone.

The beasts have been released into the cave.

The woman beside me is tugging on my coat. In the gloom I see her for the first time—pale and wide-eyed, with a mane of golden hair. Black stitches slash across her lips. Black blood coats her mouth and chin. She's pointing ahead to a pair of doors.

Several of the other captives have already spotted the exit. They're worming toward it, flinging their bodies against it as their fellow prisoners are being gnawed to pieces.

The ceiling is high enough for me and the woman to run bent over, so I help her up, and we make for the exit. It's already half-covered by a pile of naked figures, but I climb the mound of captives struggling to escape, and I drag the woman with me. I crush limbs under my boots, toss bodies aside with merciless force. Moments ago I felt a faint sense of responsibility toward these hapless prisoners, but that feeling drowns in my desperation to save this *one*. I am brutal in my determination, ruthless with my strength.

At last I have the handle of the door cleared. I turn it, shove with all my might, and it opens outward.

Strangely, none of the captives tumble through into the sunlight beyond. They're trying to get through, but some magical, invisible wall holds them inside the cave, trapped even with salvation in sight.

I grab the woman and shove her through the exit. Then I throw myself after her.

A riot of voices greets our escape—some cheering, some taunting. The sudden glare is too much for me. The sky overhead was dark when I started the maze, and yet we've tumbled into bright daylight.

The woman lies under me, her darkly golden lashes sealed against her pale cheeks. I shift off her quickly, remove my coat, and spread it over her body. Her yellow hair is tangled, and bruises mark her limbs. But worst of all is the mask of dark blood across her mouth, jaw, and throat.

Someone is approaching...a tall woman with white hair and indigo eyes, clad in a gown of lavender icicles. She's spinning a small cloud of snowflakes above her palm.

I have no idea who she is, or where I am. Quickly I survey the land around us—a wide valley, covered in snow. The trees along the valley's edge have summer leaves, but they're all encased in ice, and snowflakes shiver in the air as if they stagnated on their way to the ground. Beyond the trees, I glimpse the walls of a great fortress.

Not far away stand tiers of frozen seats filled with onlookers wearing white goggles. Behind me lies the door to the maze. All I can see of the maze itself is a large building of solid white ice, a few stories high. It doesn't look big enough to have contained all the corridors and pitfalls I navigated. It must continue underground as well, or perhaps some of what I witnessed was an illusion created by magic.

Magic. I can recall the concept, but I feel as if I'm missing huge chunks of information about who can wield it, and how. Clearly the woman walking toward us has magic. She can control water in the form of ice and snow. Frowning, I glance down at my own hands, sensing a twinge of something—power, or potential.

"Well done, Favorite," says the white-haired woman, a scornful twist in her tone. "You saved her, against all odds."

A compulsive shudder runs through my body at her voice. It is not the voice I need. This voice is cruel and cold. The white-haired woman appears to be in charge of this place and of the maze, which means she is responsible for the death of those captives, and for the mutilation of the lovely human I rescued.

I narrow my eyes at the icy woman. "You hurt my guide."

"You don't know her. Why should you care?"

I stare at the unconscious face of the girl, stained with blood and bruises, marred with black stitches of poisoned thread. "She loves me."

"How do you know?" The icy woman's voice carries a vicious kind of pain. "How do you always fucking *know*?"

"I don't understand—" I begin, but with a reckless scream she strikes me, her white claws slashing my face. One of the claws cuts across my right eye, and the vision in that eye winks out.

I bow over the woman I rescued, my blood dripping onto the red coat that covers her body.

The crowd quiets—startled, perhaps, by the icy woman's outburst.

From my right, another Fae approaches—a big male with green feathered wings. "Perhaps the winners of the Lúbra should be given a small reward, my Lady?" he ventures. "They could be healed and fed, and allowed a short time together before the next round of—entertainment?"

The Lady rounds on him with a snarl, her claws twitching. The big male withdraws a step.

"Only a suggestion," he falters. "Your guests might like to see that making it through the Lúbra is a triumph, to be rewarded by their Banríon. Otherwise no one will try to win, and then we'll be truly starved for amusement." He smiles, but it's a crooked grin, stiff with fear.

"Very well," snaps the Lady. "Take them to the kitchens, where she can be healed. Fix her, and let them fuck if they wish. Then we will test them again."

She whirls and soars away on a storm of snow.

The big winged male approaches and sinks to one knee at my side. "Shall I carry her for you? We have to walk there—" he points to the large fortress above the treetops— "to Griem Dorcha. And you look exhausted."

"No." The word is a harsh rasp, spat through my own blood and torn lips. "I will carry her. She is mine."

He nods, palms out in a deprecating gesture. "Fair is fair. I'll walk with you and see to it that you are healed."

"What is this place?" I slur through my wounded mouth. "Who are you? Who am I? Why is this happening?"

The winged male frowns. "You don't remember me?"

"I don't remember anything except the maze."

"Fuck." He rubs his forehead and sighs. "I am called Raptor. The one you're carrying is Rosebud. She named me."

The fact that he knows my woman, and that she named him—it makes me hate him with an unreasonable passion. But I restrain myself, and instead of reacting I gather the girl silently in my arms and begin walking toward the fortress.

"You're called Raven," offers Raptor helpfully, matching my stride.

"Who named me?"

"The Lady. The Banríon. The icy one." He winces. "You're her Favorite."

"What does that mean? Why am I here, and why was I put in that maze?"

"I'm not sure," he replies. "I haven't been here much longer than you have. I do know that the Lady is testing you. I don't know why, or how it involves *her*—" he gestures to the girl in my arms— "but the Lady seems to have taken your memories. I had no idea she could do that." His voice fades, and his frown deepens. "I wonder—ah!" He makes a sharp sound as if someone poked him in the ribs with a dagger. The next second his frown smooths over and he assumes a pleasant, placid expression. "Let's get you to the kitchens for some healing! No pain, only pleasure!"

I think he's mad. But since I have no choice, I follow him anyway.

18

LOUISA

We're both healed. Physically, at least.

Lir's lacerated eye has been mended, and my torn lips have been repaired. Neither of us spoke while the Twins worked over us in the kitchens of Griem Dorcha.

We're each given a bowl of stew, which Fintan assures me quietly is venison, not human. In between glances at Lir, I look around the kitchens for the royal guards, our escorts on the road. But I don't recognize any of the three Fae who bustle furtively from the cellar to the stove and back again.

What if our guards were among the captives who perished in the cave? What if they were eaten, screaming, while Lir and I escaped?

I can't think about that, or I'll vomit, and I desperately need food. So I force myself to keep eating the stew, and to put all other concerns aside for the moment.

Afterward, Raptor escorts us to a room I haven't seen before, whose main feature is a giant four-poster bed overburdened with white pillows. There's a huge rectangular mirror over the bureau, which reflects the entire bed, and an oval mirror on the ceiling. Two plush robes have been draped over a chair, but I pay no attention to them. The soft tunic I'm wearing is all I need.

Lir is dressed in a loose, velvety tunic of midnight blue, with white lounge pants. He walks into the room like a man in a dream. When Raptor leaves and closes the door with a wink, Lir just stands there, his arms hanging limply at his sides.

"We could lie down," I suggest. "I'm exhausted, and I'm sure you're tired too."

"Are you going to tell me who we are?" The twin snowflakes sparkle in his green eyes.

"I can't."

His jaw tightens and his nostrils flare. "If you love me, as you claim to, you'd find a way to explain."

Irritation tinged by despair flickers in my heart. "You're doubting me *now*? After all that?"

"What is your relationship with the green-winged fellow, Raptor?"

"He's a friend."

"A *friend*." His lip curls.

"I can have friends," I retort. "Even if you and I are—" But the spell pulls me up short, halts the words on my tongue. *Even if you and I are married.* "You don't have to be jealous."

"Don't I? When everyone else knows you better than I do? When you claim to love me but I can't remember meeting you?"

He grips my shoulders. "What the fuck happened to me? Where did I come from? Why are we here?"

I shake my head, tears springing to my eyes. "I can't tell you. I want to, but the words won't come."

"Bullshit."

I wrench myself away from him, suddenly incensed. "You have no idea what I've been through! You don't fucking understand what this has been like. It's been *torture*. You have no right to be angry with *me*. Be angry with the Banríon, with the Twins, with anyone else. Not me. You stop this, right now. Accept it, and try to function with what you know. Take advantage of the little time we have—"

He grabs me again, walks me backward to the bed, and flings me onto it. He's astride my hips in a second, pushing the tunic up to my waist. "Take advantage… like this?" he snarls. "This is what you want, right? You want me to fuck you. Ignore everything that I'm thinking and feeling, every burden I'm carrying, and *fuck you*. Make you feel special, and important, and comforted, and eased, while I still carry the burden—ahh—" He winces, puts a hand to his forehead as if he suffered a sharp pain.

I lie still beneath him, shocked by his vehemence. Some of what he said—it almost sounds like he remembers. Or maybe these emotions run so deep they can surface even without his memories.

While he's momentarily distracted, I heave myself up and flip us both over, pinning him to the bed. I grasp his wrists and glare into his face. "You'll never be free from burdens. There will always be something weighing you down, distracting you, taking you away from me—from *us*. All I want is for you to learn to put those tasks and worries aside sometimes, and enjoy your life. To really be with me, not just going through the motions. I need you *there*. I need you *present*. There has to be a balance. Yes, I would love to have all your attention all the time, but that's more than I need. I'm willing to compromise, to meet you halfway—but I need *all* of you to meet me halfway, not half of you—gods, I don't know what I'm saying, I just—"

Lir grabs the back of my neck. Drags my mouth down to his for a crushing, searing, angry kiss.

I break away, breathless. "Are you *listening* to me? I feel like you're never fully listening, like your mind is always racing away somewhere else."

"I listened in the maze, and I'm listening now."

"But you won't remember." Hot, wretched tears squeeze from my eyes. "After this, who knows what she'll do to us. I just wish... fuck, I need..."

Lir sits up, pushes me off him, and rises from the bed. Eyes blazing, he shucks off his shirt and pants. "Take that off," he orders, pointing at my tunic. "Now."

I leap up, pull the garment over my head, and throw it aside. He charges me, rams me against the wall, his hands sweeping roughly over my body, claiming it. He squeezes my breasts, sucks the nipple of one so hard that I whimper. He caresses the swell of my stomach, presses the plump mound of flesh right above my pussy, then plunges his fingers between my thighs. When I choke out a gasp, he grabs one of my legs beneath the knee and hoists it higher so I'm open to him.

Then he wedges his cock inside me, and he fucks me ferociously against the wall. Every thrust makes a soft scream burst from my throat.

He's not kissing me. He's scowling at me, truly furious, sick with lust and rage.

"I hate you for not trying hard enough to explain this," he snarls.

"I hate you for not trying hard enough, *ever*," I sob through gritted teeth. "I've always been the one trying. Trying to get your attention, trying to keep it, trying to be enough while still being myself, trying to please everyone and be what they expect me to be—gods, I'm sick of trying."

He pulls back, rams his cock into me with a vicious thrust. "I'm sick of feeling alone. Feeling as if I must hold everything inside myself, remaining always in control, always wise, always understanding—godstars—my head—" He sucks in a gasp of pain. "I can feel it there, the truth—but I can't reach it. I feel the heaviness of *everything*, and I carry it all, and still they want more of me, more and more, and *you* want more, and I *can't*—"

Teeth clenched, he shoves in harder, and I sob again, broken and blissful at the same time. My body is incandescent with heat, lust, and reckless anger, and I'm dripping, I'm clenching, I'm almost coming. I'm crying because he doesn't remember and yet he *does,* because we're both hurting and we're both right and also we are both so wrong.

Lir slams both palms against the wall. Pummels his cock into me until I'm shrieking, sore and soaring and trembling on a knife's edge of ecstasy. Then he lowers his head to my neck and *bites.*

I come as his fangs sink in.

I come like a crack of thunder, like a sheet of white-hot lightning. I come as he begins to drink my blood, just like he used to.

His name is in my mouth, but I can't speak it. I scream soundlessly, bucking my hips, and he groans against my neck and comes inside me with a compulsive tremor. As my blood flows down his throat, his cum surges into my body.

The second wave explodes over us both, the Chosen bond bathing us in dazzling, incomprehensible pleasure. My lungs won't work. For a second I think my heart stopped, but it's there, pounding away.

Lir unlatches from my neck and rocks his lean, hard body against my soft curves. He kisses me, lashes his bloody tongue through my mouth.

Suddenly his ear twitches, and he turns his head aside. "What was that?"

In the silence, I hear it too—the unmistakable gasping moans that follow a satisfying orgasm.

I look toward the source of the sound—the big rectangular mirror over the bureau. Its edges are glazed with frost, and more frost creeps across the glass as we watch.

That mirror must also serve as a window into the room. This whole time, we were being observed. And I think we gave the Banríon her much-coveted orgasm.

Part of me is angry at having our privacy disturbed, but another part is elated, because *maybe*, now that she has achieved that goal, she'll let us go.

Lir tugs his thick cock out of me, and his cum floods after it. There's much more than usual this time. That sometimes happens when Fae males are experiencing violent emotions and a deeper connection to their partner. It can also happen when they're going into heat.

Gods, I hope that's not going to be the case with Lir. Not here, not now.

"*She* was watching us," he says.

"Does that bother you?"

"I don't think I mind if people watch sometimes," he says slowly. "But I'd like to know they're watching in advance. I like to be aware of it. This feels like a violation of something sacred."

"I don't think she cares."

"I suppose not." He licks the last drops of my blood from his lips, then opens the bureau drawers and searches around for a moment before withdrawing a silken scarf. Carefully he wraps the scarf around my neck. It's snug enough to act as a bandage but not so snug as to choke me.

With that done, he lies down on his stomach on the left side of the bed—the side he prefers at home, with his head turned to the right, toward me.

I put on one of the robes and recline beside him.

Even though I'm next to him, he's not really looking at me. He's staring at nothing, his eyes hollow and tormented.

"You know I don't hate you," he murmurs.

"I know."

He sighs deeply, heavily.

At the sound of that weary sigh, pain grips my heart like a vise. He is sweetly, suddenly, infinitely precious to me. I bend over him as he lies there with half his face pressed into the sheets, and I slip my fingers into the short, silky waves of his dark hair. I kiss the black brow arched over his green eye. I trace the line of his straight nose, the angle of his cheekbone, the bow of his lips.

He doesn't respond. Keeps staring ahead, occasionally blinking his dark lashes.

I trail my fingers down his neck, to his bare shoulders. My palm brushes over his shoulder blades, along his back. I press the bumps of his spine lightly and feel him shiver when I reach the twin curves of his ass.

He hasn't been still for me like this in so long. Whenever we had sex, he always had to hurry off afterward. Always had something to do. I've never been one for cuddling, but it bothered me a little, the way he'd rise almost immediately and tend to some task.

I bend and place a kiss low on his spine, right where the crease of his ass begins.

Still he doesn't respond.

He doesn't remember me. Doesn't want this attention from me. I'm doing it again—pushing myself on him when I shouldn't.

Sighing, I end the contact with his skin and start to rise from the bed.

But his hand flashes out, grips my wrist. "Please."

I hold my breath, and for once, instead of speaking, I wait.

"Please," Lir murmurs. "Please keep touching me."

19

LOUISA

I'm getting very tired of waking up in strange places.

I remember lying on the bed with Lir. Being with him. Touching him. My caress seemed to calm whatever storm whirled in his mind.

It hurt me that I physically could not speak the words I wanted to say, to explain what happened to us and why he felt so lost. I remember that after he fell asleep, I cried silently for a long time.

I remember a servant entering the room with wine, and I drank some because I craved rest. I wanted to drink myself to sleep and be oblivious to pain for a while.

But there must have been something in that wine—a Fae concoction, magic, an herb—something that sent me so deep into unconsciousness that I didn't wake up until now.

I'm in a forest, dimly lit by luminous snowflakes that drift through the darkness between slim gray trunks. Overhead are dark purple leaves, trimmed with glowing frost.

The Banríon's magic is exquisite, I'll give her that. She can make ice that doesn't melt, ice that glows, ice in every conceivable shape, ice and snow in all colors. Whole buildings and mazes of ice. She's brilliant, creative, and sensitive. Devastatingly beautiful, and wickedly cruel.

I can only imagine what new horror she has concocted to test me and Lir. When will she be satisfied?

If she's only looking for physical satisfaction, I think she achieved it last night. The signs were all there. But maybe she wants to wring *more* pleasure out of us, or continue investigating our bond until she's convinced of whatever it is she's looking for.

I pick myself up out of the leaves on the forest floor. I'm wearing a white, close-fitting dress and a scarlet cloak, silk-lined. Pretty, but not necessarily the best garb for tromping through a forest.

Something crunches off to my left, then crunches again. My head whips in that direction, and for a second I gape, too shocked to comprehend what I'm seeing.

It's me.

A young woman of exactly my size and shape, dressed in the same outfit, with the same long golden braid and blue eyes. She has my nose, my round cheeks, my chin. She's *me*.

One look passes between us, and then she glances anxiously behind her and leaps into motion, bounding off through the trees like a frightened deer.

Well, shit.

So this is the next test. The Banríon has glamoured at least one person, probably more, to look like me, and Lir is supposed to, what? Find me? The girl I just saw looked terrified, like she was running from something. Maybe Lir is supposed to save me, like in the cave. Perhaps there are monsters loose in the woods, and he has to figure which one of *me* he wants to rescue.

Fuck that. I'm not trusting our Chosen bond to save my life out here—that's just silly. I won't trust luck to bring Lir to my rescue at just the right moment. I was rather an idiot about the beast that chewed its way into my room, but I intend to do better this time. I can do my own rescuing.

First things first—find a more secure place from which I can observe what's happening. If I were thinner, I could probably climb a tree and gain a vantage point that way, but all the trees in the vicinity look too slender to hold my weight. I scan the ground and find the direction where it seems to be slanting slightly upward, and I walk that way. Sure enough, the forest floor climbs to a slight ridge, studded with protruding rocks.

Hitching my dress up, I climb the largest rock, thanking my past self for all the training I've been doing and the muscle I've gained. When I reach the top, I blow on my chilled fingers to warm them and survey the forest. I haven't gained much altitude, but I can see a bit farther through the trees, which means I'll have more warning if something bad approaches.

A big fallen branch lies against the rock I'm standing on, so I reach down and grab it. After I've snapped off the extra twigs, it makes a decent cudgel.

I've got high ground and a weapon. Not much else to do but wait, and try to stay warm.

Blinking away the glowing snowflakes, I shift from one foot to the other, weighing the cudgel in my palms. Waiting.

It streaks out of the woods without warning—a dark, lean shape, furred and lanky. A wolf, maybe, or a Fae with a wolfish shape. It's scrambling up the rocks, already reaching for me with a long, furry arm. A growl ripples from its throat.

I whack the monster's arm with the cudgel, and it recoils with a snarl. Then it's climbing again, claws scrabbling on stone.

With a yell, I swing the cudgel into the side of its face.

The blow is heavy enough to knock it off the rocks. It crashes onto its side, while I scramble down the opposite side of the rockpile and run.

Fuck, I shouldn't be running, I should have stayed where I was. I'm not a fast runner. I gave up the high ground. Fuck.

Too late to second-guess myself now.

The monster howls somewhere behind me, and I gasp. Swiftly I dart aside, behind a clump of trees. I press my back to a trunk and I wait, gripping my cudgel.

A gallop of paws on the crunchy leaves. Then it stops, far too close for comfort.

The shift and press of one paw in the crunchy leaves, then another. The unmistakable sound of *sniffing*.

It's following my scent, like a hound pursuing a fox. Foxes are smart—*be smart, Louisa. Think of something.*

Slowly I bend over and quietly pluck a few loose stones from the ground. Then I hurl them into the undergrowth. At the distant thump and rustle of their impact, the monster whines with ravenous eagerness and lopes away toward the sound.

I run again, as far as I can, until I reach a grove of larger, thicker trees. Unfortunately their lowest limbs are too high for me to reach, but one of the biggest trunks is the size of a gardener's shack and has a large opening at the base of its trunk, near the roots. It almost looks as if it used to be two trees that merged into one, long ago.

The tree looks half dead, and there are luminescent blue mushrooms growing along its trunk, scenting the air with an odd, musty odor. But I'm not in any place to be picky.

As I wedge myself into the crack, I can't help recalling how Lir and I hid in a space like this, months ago. We were alone, trying to reach the Unending Pool so his nutcracker curse could be broken.

I wanted him so badly then. I craved his attention, his nearness. I hated the scornful way he spoke to me sometimes, but I craved it, too, like one might crave the heat of spice in an otherwise bland dish. When we hid in the hollow of that tree, I asked him to bite me again. But I wanted more than that, and he knew it.

I tilt my head back against the ridged trunk and close my eyes for a moment, remembering that conversation like it was yesterday.

"Why, Lir? Why are you so afraid to admit that you want me? From what I've heard, plenty of Fae sleep with humans. There's nothing forbidden about it."

"But I don't merely want to sleep with you!" he said. *"Gods, I thought when you hid your scent I would get some relief but—it never ends, this battle I must fight when I'm around you. Remember when I said you smell like food and sex?"*

"Yes."

"To me you smell like more. Your scent... it's like nothing else I've ever encountered. It's tailored to me, designed to be the one fragrance I can't resist. That's how I heard my father describe it when he found his Chosen. My mother."

And then he explained what he meant by that word: Chosen.

"The royal Fae may encounter multiple potential mates with such a scent in their lifetime, or none at all. It is not a fated pairing, no forceful hand of destiny—but the scent draws two

beings together. And if they should find love, they may become each other's Chosen. It is a bond no others in Faerie experience, only the reigning ruler and their selected mate. And that bond brings with it a more exquisite pleasure, a more abiding loyalty, and a more fulfilling love than most Fae or humans will ever know."

I think he had too narrow a view of the Chosen bond then, or perhaps his father misinformed him. Clearly the "reigning ruler and their selected mate" aren't the only Fae who can experience such a bond, since the Banríon herself had a mate bond in the past. Perhaps Lir's father had an exclusive view of such things and believed that only the monarch of the land could experience a *true* bond. But maybe others of royal blood can experience one, too, and Lir's father simply did not wish to acknowledge that.

Even as my ears strain for any sounds of the wolf returning to hunt me, my mind continues replaying what Lir told me on that night, months ago.

"I thought the scent of you was the only thing compelling me—luring me to obsess over you. But your scent is concealed from me now, and I still have these feelings—this inner dread at the thought of losing you, this ache, even when you're near me, because you're not close enough, because I need you—not your body, not only that, but more. I admire you, Louisa. I admire your confidence, your keen mind, your beautiful enthusiasm for everything, your courage in crisis. I long to be like you. I wish I could lose myself entirely in you. I know I tried to frighten you about life in Faerie—I wanted you to leave, because then I might get some relief from this agony. I told you if you stayed, your life would be cut short. I can't promise that won't be true, but I can promise to stand between you and every danger if you'll stay, if

you'll only let me hold you once in a while, and if you will stroke my hair sometimes, like you did tonight."

I was flattered, yes, but I was frightened, too, especially when he said, *"My heart chose you the moment your blood touched me, the moment I sprang to life in your hands. I fought against it—stars, I fought so hard. My head kept telling me you were a foolish choice, ill-suited for life at my side, as Queen. But you have proven me wrong, so many times. I am the ill-suited one. You—you are incredible. You are my Chosen."*

After that confession of his—after he tore open his chest and laid his heart bare before me, I let my fear take over, and I said words that I would withdraw now, if I could. *"This isn't what I wanted. I just wanted to fuck you."*

He went silent then. Didn't speak to me about it again until we met up with his royal guards, until he came to me in my tent. He apologized to me, something the Fae rarely do, and I've carried that apology in my heart. *"I am sorry for the things I've said to you since we met, Louisa. No matter what pain and confusion I felt, I had no right to cut into your heart with my words. I understand if you cannot forgive it. But I am asking one more time if you could love me, if you think you could choose me. If you do not, and you cannot, I will leave you alone. I won't make any more confessions, or disturb you on this topic again."*

I told him my fear, that I would grow tired of our bond and end up hurting him. And he said, *"Loving someone is baring your heart to pain. I understand that, and I accept it. If you choose me, and then later you tire of me, I will not hold you back from seeking your joy. But let me assure you, the Chosen bond provides the keenest pleasure known to my kind. I don't believe you'd find anyone else satisfying once you've experienced it with me. That's what I've heard, anyway. You wanted me, tempted me. You have me. Now it's your decision. Choice is freedom."*

And I chose, in that moment. Impulsively, I chose him. I accepted the bond and willingly stepped into his life.

Did I really understand what it meant? No. Did I truly know him? Of course not—I'd only just met him.

Did that impulsivity, that lack of understanding—did it make my choice any less sincere?

No.

I meant it then, and I mean it now.

Lir is mine. He has been mine since I first picked up the nutcracker in Drosselmeyer's house. He fascinated me even then. And when I dropped him, when I saw him lying there on the floor, with that sliver broken from his arm—my heart responded. I couldn't rest until I had fixed him, not just because he was a creation of my godfather, but because something about him called to me. Summoned me.

I've never thought about it quite like that before. He was in another form, under a terrible curse, and I couldn't stop thinking about him, wanting to mend his damage.

Perhaps I chose him first, after all.

I've been out here for hours, near as I can tell, and I'm shivering with cold despite the cloak. I curl in on myself, trying to pretend I can feel heat spreading through my limbs, when in reality my toes are going numb. I wiggle them desperately inside my boots.

I'm so hungry that I'm beginning to think very seriously of plucking and devouring a few of the mushrooms growing along the lip of the tree's hollow. But brightly colored glowing things generally mean *poison* in the human realm, and from what I've seen, things aren't so different in Faerie.

There's a trembling weakness in my legs and arms, born from exertion and lack of food. How many hours has it been since I last ate?

Maybe if I manage to kill the wolf-monster, I can eat it, although honestly I'd much prefer a large slice of cake. Not dry, crumbly cake with raisins like the kind my father used to buy for me and Clara on our birthdays—moist, flavorful cake with smooth, thick frosting, like the kind we'd order in secret from the local bakery when our father was especially occupied with business. I used to pinch coins from the bag he kept to pay the milkman, the farrier, and our occasional tutors. Those salvaged coins lived at the bottom of a button box, and I called them our "happiness fund." What I wouldn't give to eat a slice of that cake—to sink my teeth through a layer of creamy frosting, into that dense, rich, delicious—

Somewhere in the forest, I hear a shriek. Goosebumps break out all over my body as a deathly chill runs up my spine. I stay motionless, hoping the wolf-monster will be satisfied with his kill and not come after me. It's a horrible thought, and I'm probably wicked for thinking it. But if it's between me and some glamoured lookalike Fae I don't know…

Wait…

What is that? An odd sound near me, at the level of my ear. A low, heavy, hoarse, repetitive sound.

It's the sound of something *breathing*. Something *big*. And it's sitting right next to the tree I'm hiding in.

Immediately, instinctively, I hold my own breath.

The thing sitting beside my tree couldn't have been the cause of that faraway scream. Which means there is more than one dangerous beast in these woods. Raptor mentioned there was good hunting around Griem Dorcha, but he never specified *what* they hunt.

The heavy panting continues. It sounds doglike. Wolflike. A thick, hungry, harsh, bestial breathing.

My cold fingers curl tighter around my weapon.

Why is it just sitting there? It must be able to smell me. Or maybe the strange odor of the mushrooms is blending with my scent, confusing the creature.

My lungs are getting tight, so I part my lips and release the breath I was holding as silently as I can.

The panting changes, speeds up. The rhythm is almost sexual.

If Clara were here, if she knew what I was thinking right now, she'd raise her eyebrows. *Why are you thinking about sex at a time like this? There couldn't be a more inappropriate moment.*

And just to shock her, I'd reply, *Because I'm sex-obsessed. I think about it all the fucking time. It's who I am.*

I imagine the prim, horrified look she'd give me. Or perhaps she wouldn't be horrified, after all. Since she met Fin, she has become much naughtier and more adventurous, or so I've gathered from the hints Fin drops on occasion. In fact, I think their sex life has been more exciting than mine and Lir's. At least, until this trip.

Gods, my brain—it's going off track again when I'm in danger. I need to stay focused. Survive. Rescue myself.

The heavy breathing continues, and the snow begins to fall more thickly, bits of blue luminous fluff in the darkness. That's all I can see, and I don't dare poke my head outside the crack to look around.

But I can't stay here forever, either. My body is buzzing with nervous energy, and I recall the time when Lir and I hid from the giant mole-rat and we had to stay very, very still, and I *couldn't*. I wasn't built for hiding. I need to flee or fight.

Slowly I shift my position, just a little. Just enough to get my arms in a better position to strike if I see any sign of the wolf.

Just one little movement.

A wolfish face bursts through the swirling snow, into my hollow. I jab my cudgel at the monster with a scream, striking its muzzle. It pulls back just enough for me to lunge out of the hollow tree and roll aside.

I'm on my feet instantly, running. But even with glimmering flakes of snow giving me a little light, running in the woods at night is fucking dangerous. I smash my toe against a rock within seconds and fly headlong into the undergrowth.

I roll over and scramble backward on my butt until my spine hits a tree. I've lost my cudgel. Fuck.

A low growl trickles through the cold gloom, and I glimpse a huge wolflike form pacing behind the tree trunks.

It's right there. Watching me. Stalking me.

Hauling myself up, I run again, straight through a patch of thorns this time. They catch on my cloak, tangling me up until I have to unpin the garment and leave it behind.

On I run, dragging in frigid lungfuls of air, puffing out heated breath into the night. Pain twinges along my right side, just under my ribs, and my thighs are shaking.

I pause and bend over, desperate for a deep breath, but I can't seem to summon one. I'm gasping, but the air doesn't go all the way to the bottom of my lungs like I so desperately need it to.

"Shit," I sob. Between my fear and the physical exertion, my heart is pounding at a frightening speed. I need to calm down, but who could be calm when they're being hunted?

Finally I manage to draw a satisfying breath, and I hurry on. It's more of a limping jog than a run this time, and yet I still manage to misstep and tumble down a slope. More thorns. Jagged rocks. I tear myself free, ripping off half my skirt and part of one sleeve in the process. My legs are bruised, my hands and arms bleeding, and still I run.

I need shelter. Another weapon. High ground. Help.

A half-frozen stream glimmers in the starlight and snowlight. As I'm preparing to jump over it, a huge shape rockets out of the dark and slams into my chest. I'm knocked flat, pinned by a hulking beast with long gangly legs and sharp-nailed paws.

The wolf looms above my face, his pointed ears and shaggy shoulders silhouetted against the cold indigo sky and the gray clouds. The falling snow dances like tiny blue fireflies around his hulking shape.

Lowering his muzzle, he snuffles along my cheek, then along the curve of my neck. A low chuff of satisfaction breaks from him, and his long tongue slides out, wetly caressing my face.

I cringe and twist away, preparing to buck him off, but he settles his weight on top of me.

And then he fucking *lies down* on my body.

The strange thing is, even though I'm still scared, that firm weight settles me. Especially when the wolf-monster places both forepaws on my breasts and rests his muzzle between them, his furry brows twitching as he watches my face.

He's not attacking me.

I stay there, motionless, while the warmth of his body seeps into mine. The snow has slackened again; it's barely flurries now.

After a few minutes the wolf nuzzles his damp nose harder against one of my breasts, then begins licking the exposed skin enthusiastically.

"That's fucking strange," I whisper.

He whines, tucks his muzzle against the tender skin beneath my ear, and sighs with a kind of weary relief.

Slowly I lift my hand and lay it against the side of his neck. His fur is black, glossy, almost wavy in places, and softer than I expected.

Another scream echoes through the woods. The wolf lifts his head sharply, ears twitching.

Then he looks down at me.

At that moment, the clouds shift, and rays of moonlight bathe us both, illuminating his eyes, showing me their color for the first time.

Green eyes, with snowflakes in the center.

The clash of emotions is too much for me. Horror, shock, joy, grief, hope, fear—I can't handle it, and I freeze.

I stare at him.

He whines again, a faint whistle of yearning and sorrow from his wolf-throat, and he licks my cheek.

Lir.

He doesn't know me. Doesn't remember. And yet he's *here*.

In this form, his attraction to me isn't about fate, or fucking, or my appearance, or even the way I smell, because I'd bet my palace the Banríon copied my scent somehow and doused my doppelgangers with it. There are women running through this forest who have been glamoured to look like me and probably smell like me, and yet here he is.

"You beautiful, impossible bastard," I choke out. Gently I push him back so I can sit up. He shifts to sit on his haunches beside me, panting through his long jaws, watching me expectantly.

"We need to go back to the Banríon," I tell him. "Do you understand anything I'm saying? Do you know how to find her?"

Lir's eyes are his, but they're empty of everything except an open, innocent, puppyish affection. He doesn't understand.

But when I rise and walk a few steps away, he growls.

Cautiously I turn back. The ruff along his neck and shoulders bristles with aggression. His head is lowered, his ears are pinned back, and his teeth are bared. The warning is unmistakable. If I run, he will chase me. If I try to leave, he'll ensure that I stay.

I'm debating what to do when a sound slices through the quiet of the night—a keen, piercing whistle, cold as the winter wind.

Instantly the wolf's ears prick up. He bounds forward through the light blanket of snow coating the leaves, then looks back and chuffs at me. It's clear he wants me to follow him.

I don't need to be told who is summoning him, and I hate that he's obeying her. But he's headed where I need to go, and my place is with him anyway, no matter what form either of us may take.

This wolf form must be temporary, surely. The Banríon wouldn't leave him like this.

But I never specified that he must be in human form when she set us free.

This is why you don't make bargains with faeries, Louisa, you fucking idiot.

As I stumble through the forest after the Lir-wolf, I think of all the different ways I could have worded our bargain better. All the loopholes I could have closed. I simply didn't think of all the angles. My brain, so good at strategy and rapid analysis, failed me.

As Lir and I walk through the trees, I hear the sound of running feet. One of my doppelgangers races past us, sobbing frantically. A snarl rips through the night, and two great shapes bound after her, jaws wide and slavering. The wolves leap on her, fangs sinking into her shoulders as they bear her down to the ground and begin tearing into her flesh. Her glamour shivers and breaks, revealing a Fae with pink skin and white antlers.

I can't see her face, can't be sure, but I think she was one of our royal guards.

With a cry I start toward her, but Lir growls, blocks my path with his body, and nudges my arm roughly. He won't let me get any closer to those wolves and their prize.

I know it's too late to save the guard, but it hurts me to leave her there. Her death settles in my heart, a dull pain worse than the ache in my weary feet.

With Lir loping beside me, I manage to keep up a decent pace, driven by the terror of those other wolves. I'm trembling more than ever now, not only from the cold and the lack of food, but from the strain on my nerves.

The cold is growing worse. And the farther we walk, the thicker the snow becomes, swirling down in blinding white eddies between the trees. The wind shears between the tree trunks and howls in the tossing branches. It's almost as if the forest's temper is rising.

Glittering icicles form on limbs above us, dropping with lethal suddenness. Lir and I have to jump aside to avoid them. One slashes my upper arm, another slices the back of my hand.

Is the Banríon trying to test us, or kill us?

Finally the deadly icicles stop falling, but the snowstorm heightens, with screaming winds so ferocious I have to slow to a painful trudge. The Lir-wolf comes up beside me, nudging under my arm. He's so tall I can lean on his shoulders a little.

At last, at long, long last, I see open land ahead. We are almost out of the woods.

When we step out from the eaves of the forest, I have to shield my face from the biting wind and driving snow. My fingers hurt so badly from the cold, I can hardly bear it. Before us the ground slopes up, right to the wall of Griem Dorcha. A few trees stand at intervals between the forest and the wall, and beneath one of those ice-clad trees is the Banríon. Long claws like icicles extend from her hands while reckless, magnificent magic flows out of her.

The Twins cower behind her, clutching each other as the snowstorm rages, watching me and Lir with pity and horror in their eyes. There are no other witnesses this time.

The Lir-wolf takes my wrist gently in his mouth and tugs me toward the Banríon, like a pet bringing his owner the trophy of his hunt.

"This is a fucking joke." A vicious smile trembles on the Banríon's lips. She stares at the Lir-wolf, her eyes wild, enraged. "They all looked like her, sounded like her, smelled like her—and you've brought me *her*. How? How the fuck? How do you always know?"

As she screams at him, the Lir-wolf releases my wrist and shrinks backward. The Twins step forward, and Fintan grips Lir's head, immobilizing it while Fionn opens his jaws and pulls out his tongue. The spell must be written there, an invisible inkblood charm for full-body shifting. As Lir whines, Fionn slits the back of her brother's wrist, dips her quill in his blood, and unwrites the spell.

The instant she's done, the wolf transforms into Lir. Even though I knew it was him, a thrill passes through my stomach at the revelation.

He stands motionless, his dark head bowed in the face of the Banríon's wrath.

"You don't deserve this bond, either of you," she roars, black tears streaming down her cheeks. "Not you, the royal-blooded weakling who practically begs for subjugation, and not the human whore whose reek makes you salivate. It doesn't make sense, any of it. You're tricking me somehow, you're playing with me, mocking me. I hate myself for enjoying the sight of your antics last night...I hate both of you, you wretched, oozing *worms*..."

The Banríon's claws elongate and she stabs the four fingers of her right hand into Lir's neck.

I shriek and lunge forward, but the Twins seize my arms and hold me back.

Lir chokes, spitting blood, scratching at the Banríon with his own claws, but she doesn't falter. She drags him by his neck, down the slope, to a flat space right at the edge of the forest.

"What is she doing?" I sob out, wrenching against the Twins' hold.

"She'll kill you," Fintan says, and Fionn murmurs, "Best to stay here."

"No, no!" I struggle with the dregs of my strength, but I'm weary, wounded, starved—I have almost nothing left. I can't get free. Can't help him.

The Banríon throws Lir to the ground on his back, encasing his legs and upper arms in ice to immobilize him. Spikes of ice manifest in her hands, and she plunges them into his eyes, his ears, his nostrils—as she yanks out his tongue and slashes it off with the razor edge of an ice-blade. She grips his hand at the wrist, cuts off his fingertips. Does the same to his other hand.

I'm screaming, roaring, hoarse and helpless and dying inside, shrieking curses against the Banríon, fighting the iron grip of the Twins. I feel like my heart is going to explode, like the horror and urgency swelling in my body is going to fucking kill me, like she's killing him.

If he Fades, I will die.

Finally the Banríon backs away from Lir's mangled body, her chest heaving. "You cannot touch, smell, see, taste, or hear her!" she shouts over the howling wind. The ice around Lir's legs creaks and flexes, and I hear bones crack. He cries out, agonized, through his tongueless mouth.

"And you cannot walk," she says, furiously gleeful. "Let's see you find your precious Chosen now!" She shatters the ice that binds his body, then kicks him over onto his stomach, into the ever-thickening blanket of snow on the ground.

With frenzied purpose in her eyes, she marches up the slope toward me.

As the Banríon draws nearer, the Twins fall back, leaving me to my fate. I stagger forward, expecting to die, hoping to get in one good punch before I do.

But the Banríon doesn't kill me. She creates a chain of black ice around my wrist and anchors it to a nearby tree. I lunge against the chain, desperate to hurt her, but she's out of my reach.

"Stay, and watch him suffer," she says.

"You're so fucking wicked," I seethe at her. "Despite your title, you're no ruler—just a cowardly abuser. I'm more of a queen than you'll ever be. I pitied you once, but I despise you now. You hate what you don't understand, and you hate us for possessing what you never had. You're a bitter, jealous, fucking *cunt.*"

"And you're going to die out here," she says with a rictus grin. "You'll freeze to death. And he might die as well. If he manages to recover, you'd best believe I'm going to make him fuck me until he cums blood. Restraint is sickeningly overrated."

With a snap of her fingers to the Twins, she strides back toward Griem Dorcha. The Twins follow her meekly, casting sympathetic looks back at me. I despise their pity. It isn't true bravery or empathy. It doesn't help me or Lir. They are weak cowards in service to a brutal queen.

Once she calms down, she may regret her words and actions. She might relent soon enough to spare our lives and bring us both back inside, within the shelter of the prison. But I will never place the slightest trust in her again. The damaged yet reasonable woman I met has allowed her jealousy, bitterness, and despair to drown all wisdom and logic, as well as the shreds of mercy she once possessed.

The storm she summoned doesn't lessen when she leaves. If anything, it grows worse. Snow thickens, tossed in wild eddies by the freezing wind, until I can't see Lir's crumpled body at all.

My tears have frozen on my cheeks. I can feel them crackling against my skin. Snowflakes clump on my eyelashes, and I blink them away. I'm shaking with the cold, but at least I'm not entirely numb yet.

I try to scream Lir's name, but the inkblood bargain won't let me. He wouldn't be able to hear me anyway, not after she stabbed those icy spikes into his ears. I don't know how long it might take him to heal naturally from those wounds, without any potions or spells. The rate of healing is different for each Fae, and sometimes, if the wounds are bad enough and their energy is too low, they can Fade, even from wounds that shouldn't be mortal.

My mate could be dying out there in the snow, right now. Sightless, voiceless, unable to hear or walk, he could be Fading, turning gray. Cracks will branch through his body and he'll crumble into ashes while I sit here, chained to this tree.

I'm going to him. I don't care if I have to break my wrist and tear off my hand. The Banríon's icy chain may be unbreakable, but I'm not.

I'm mentally preparing myself for the effort, for the agony, when I see a dark shape through the swirling snow. Something low and lumpy. Something...

It's Lir. Crawling up the hill, through the snow, his mutilated fingers leaving streaks of scarlet on white. He's hauling his body along on his forearms and elbows, broken legs dragging behind him. His eyes are sightless. Blood trickles from his ears and nose, stains his jaw. And yet he's headed straight for me.

And I fucking *break*.

In some place deeper than my heart, right at the core of my being, I break, and I bleed.

"Why don't you quit?" I cry out, even though I know he can't hear me. "Why won't you stop loving me, when I've done nothing to deserve it? There's no reason for you to choose me, to want me this badly. I'm not worthy."

He's still dragging himself toward me. Closer, and closer. I crawl to the very end of my chain and reach toward him.

"I choose *you*," I scream through a sob. "I fucking choose you, and I'll do it over and over as long as I live. I promise, darling, I promise."

His trembling, damaged fingers slide over my knee. He moves forward a little farther. Lays his tortured head in my lap.

And I bow over that precious head, wrapping my arms around that bloodstained face, sobbing, breaking.

"You love me beyond sense, beyond reason, and beyond fate," I whisper to him. "Your love is relentless. And so is mine."

He shifts a little, turning his face up to the sky, and as I weep, hot tears fall from my eyes straight into his.

The moment those tears land, the snowflakes on his ruined irises flash with a green glow.

I've seen that glow before, that specific hue. It's the color of a curse breaking.

I gasp, still leaning over him, letting two more of my tears drip onto his eyes.

And the snowflakes melt away, leaving only clear green.

Lir blinks.

Looks at me.

There's a moment of frozen clarity between us, of realization. I can see his mind racing, running through the retrieved memories, sorting them all out, sizing up the situation.

Recognizing me.

Then... remembering who he is.

A Lord of Faerie. King of the Seelie.

That title comes with a magnificent birthright, a power unimaginable to those who haven't witnessed it—especially when the kingdom is being threatened. I don't know how long we've been at Griem Dorcha, but our entire stay has been one long attack on his safety and wellbeing. And when he is under attack, so is the kingdom. Which means he can draw upon that deeper well of energy that lies within him, access speedier healing powers, and summon the most dramatic abilities in his possession.

He's already healing, right before my eyes. His fingertips are growing back. His ragged ears heal, and the blood evanesces from his skin. His nostrils quiver, and as his tongue reforms he opens his mouth and says, "Louisa."

Then his eyes widen with shock and guilt. "Godstars, I slept with someone else—"

"No!" I interrupt, clasping his hand. "You didn't. It was me, every time. I'll explain everything, but right now, we're in danger."

"From the Banríon." He sits up, nods grimly, and adjusts one of his broken legs with a sickening snap so it will heal straight. "Fuck that bitch."

I choke out a laugh that's partly a sob. There's a strange sensation along my back—the spell Fintan wrote on me is evanescing, allowing me the freedom to say anything to Lir again, since a key condition of the bargain has changed.

"I think your memories are safe now," I tell him. "And I don't think you'll lose them when we leave. From what I understand, the spell that stole them is like a wall around this place, and it only affects people coming in. The Banríon said everyone else's memory loss is permanent. You only got yours back because I'm your mate, and we're connected, so your memories were suppressed, not destroyed, but some of our guards are dead, maybe all of them, and—"

"Louisa." His voice is deep, tender, and it gently hushes my frantic babbling. He cups my face with one hand. With the other he grasps my chain and crumbles it into dust. "Sweetheart, you've been so strong. I can't even imagine what you've endured—"

"It's over," I whisper, tears welling up again. "It's all over now."

"I remember what you said last night. I haven't been there for you. I hurt you, I was selfish—"

"No. *No.*" I pull his head up, clasp his face between my hands, desperate for him to understand. "Not just you. Both of us. The things I did to you when we met… I was foolish and selfish and wrong, back then and every day since. And I will be foolish and selfish and wrong again, I'm sure, but I will strive not to be, consciously *strive*. I will work at this love, because it is the best thing I've ever had." I hesitate, and then I say the bravest words I've ever spoken about myself. Words that I hope I'll fully believe one day. "In spite of every flaw, I deserve love like this, and so do you."

Lir pulls me in. Kisses me softly, and the heat of his body flows through mine, warming me, healing me like it did on that day by the Unending Pool, when I first saw his true power.

As we kiss, his form expands, growing taller and broader. He can grow up to ten times his usual height, but he doesn't go that far with it this time—only a half-size bigger. Still, he's huge, and strong, and when metallic silver dragon wings burst from his back, I feel like cheering.

He lifts me off the snowy ground, cradles me in his arms, and heads for Griem Dorcha.

20

LIR

The Banríon is waiting for us.

I believe she sensed it when my memories returned, when the bargain between her and Louisa ended. She knew I would come for her.

I remember every conversation I've had with her, including the ones Louisa doesn't know about. The Banríon told me her true name—Caitríona. Told me detailed stories from her past. She suppressed each one after she confessed it to me, but she must have guessed my memories might return one day. I believe she wanted someone to know all those things about her. To understand the long torment and shattered hopes that created the damaged soul she is today.

She wanted someone to see her. To care.

And as many of us do, she went about it the wrong way, entirely.

At the door of the Banríon's great hall, I set Louisa down. I was left naked and broken in the snow, but thanks to my Chosen, I am whole once again. I deserve clothing to match my station, and so does my queen. I'm not as skilled or creative at conjuring such things as my cousin, but I can replicate outfits I've seen and touched, so I craft a fine suit and a rich cape for myself. For Louisa I conjure a warm, long-sleeved gown to replace the ragged scraps she's wearing, and I give her a cape as well.

In this form, I tower high above my mate, yet she looks more regal than I've ever seen her—sobered, perhaps, by suffering. And though I love the serious confidence she exudes, my heart bleeds for the boisterous, sunshiny Louisa I married, and I vow to help her reclaim that side of herself once this trial has passed.

For now, I must do my duty as King, and mete out justice upon the one who has caused so much harm to me and mine.

As Louisa and I pace toward the Mirror of Reason and the Banríon's throne, I glance around at the icy tiers of seats, all empty.

"Have you sent them away, or slain them all?" I call to her.

"Many died in the Lúbra, and more in the forest during the hunt," replies the Banríon. "The rest have been sent to their quarters—all except three, who angered me by interceding for you."

Her icy claws curl into the fabric of her skirts, which are spread out far over the ice in a sea of frothy furs, glistening pearls, and billows of lace. As she gathers the fabric toward herself, it slides off three bodies lying prone upon the ice.

The Twins, their skin already gray and cracking. They are past hope.

Raptor, face-down between his pale-green wings. I cannot tell what condition he's in.

Louisa makes a strangled sound of blended grief and anger. She glances at me desperately, and when I nod, she rushes over to Raptor, using all the strength of her newly healed body to turn him over.

I continue across the ice, until I'm looming over the throne and the slender Fae within it. She looks so small now. So much less threatening than she did when my memories were trapped by her power.

To her credit, she doesn't summon any of her ice magic, or try to defend herself. She knows how quickly and decisively such a fight would end. With my memories intact, I know how to access every bit of power I possess. She might as well be a worm fighting a hawk.

"You knew it would come to this," I say.

"I suspected it might."

"Have you anything to say before the end?"

Her irises shine in pale rings against the navy orbs of her eyes. Her lips tighten at first, then tremble a little as she speaks. "Only that it isn't *fair*. It isn't just, or right. Whatever fate or godstar gave you two this glorious bond, and turned mine to poison—they deserve eternal pain for that injustice. Whatever power determined that this human girl should reign while I spent centuries in captivity, is wicked beyond measure, and supremely unfair."

Louisa speaks up, rising from her place beside Raptor. "You're right, it isn't fair. Life can be wretchedly cruel. But if you deal with your suffering by viciously passing it along to others—if you torture them, emotionally or physically, so you can feel better—that is the worst kind of weakness. I know what I'm saying, because I've done it before, many times, even to my beloved sister. I like to think I'm stronger than that now. A better person."

Louisa pauses, her breath hitching in a half-sob, her hands clenched. "At the end of your life, you could have done wonderful things with your magic, and instead you chose to steal from others, to use them, to make your final days all about yourself—your history, your suffering, the privileges you didn't enjoy. You thought the wrongs against you gave you the right to mistreat others. And so you became as bad as the ones who hurt you. Which is truly, truly heartbreaking. I feel sorry for you. But you have taught me not to take for granted the relationships I have—the love of my mate, the life I've been given to enjoy, and the responsibilities I will assume from this day forward. I feel that I've aged a decade, inside." Louisa touches her chest. "I'm wiser now. And for that, I am grateful."

The Banríon's face has grown hard as stone, cold as ice. I suspect she heard the truth of everything Louisa said, and understands that she wasted her last days. Perhaps she regrets it all—but regret at this point is too unbearable, so she is hardening herself. Preparing for the final judgment.

And I deliver it without further delay, because although this is justice for the loss and death she has caused, I take no vengeful pleasure in it.

"Caitríona, Lady of Ice, you imprisoned, threatened, and harmed the King and Queen of the Seelie. By doing so you endangered the entire kingdom. Thus your sentence is immediate death. Because of your crimes, you deserve annihilation. But if the godstars have pity upon you, they may see fit to send you to the skies, to ride with the Wild Hunt until the day you have earned your redemption. Begone now, and trouble us no more."

I do not need to lay a hand on her—my proclamation is enough. In this form, under this sort of threat, a pronouncement of death upon an enemy of the kingdom takes immediate effect.

The Banríon's skin turns a deep gray. Forked white lines spread and interconnect, deepening until she fractures into a thousand pieces. Those pieces, along with her conjured gown, collapse into powdery ash and melt away.

The ice beneath my feet vanishes. So do the throne, the rows of seats, and the decorative frost and crystals on the walls and ceiling. The hall of Griem Dorcha is plain stone once again.

"Fuck, I can hardly believe she's gone," Louisa says. "Thank the godstars."

"Thank *me*." I give her a wink and a half-smile.

She smiles back, joy lighting her eyes at my teasing. I shall have to do more teasing from now on. Perhaps Finias can give me some lessons.

"Can you heal Raptor?" she asks, her voice tentative. "He's kind. He helped me while you—while we were here."

She's uncertain, afraid I'll be jealous and let him suffer. But there's not a trace of jealousy in my heart. I'm sure there will be again—perhaps regarding that fucker Captain Dónal—but when it happens, Louisa and I will discuss it and deal with it together. For now, all I feel toward Raptor is gratitude.

Healing him is the work of a moment. When he comes to, Louisa explains things to him while I pace around the room, pondering our next move. The bodies of the Twins are disintegrating more slowly than the Banríon's did, but they will be gone in moments. Not a trace of their existence, or their unique magic, will be left behind. I can remember them now, and the conversations I overheard between them and the Banríon. They should have tried to restrain her, but instead they enabled her cruelty in the name of friendship.

Now they are barely a memory. Just a bit of dust on the floor that clings to my boots as I cross the room again.

When Louisa finishes speaking with Raptor, I walk over and address him. "How would you like to be temporarily in charge of this place?"

His eyes widen. "My King, I would be honored, but I'm no one—at least, not that I can remember."

"You're the best choice," I tell him. "You may not have your memories, but you understand what occurred here, and that knowledge can advise your governance of Griem Dorcha. I think it best not to tell anyone else that their memories were stolen. Doing so would only cause them unnecessary pain. Unfortunately, memory magic is not undone by the death of its caster. The Queen and I will return to Beannú and consult with scholars of such magic, to discover if there is any way to reverse it. The circle of memory-stealing spellwork may still be intact around the prison, so we will need experts who can detect and dismantle it. In the meantime, you can keep everyone calm and keep the place running."

Raptor bows. "I would consider it an honor. But I would rather not do it alone. May I appoint Scarlet as my second in command?"

"Look there," says Louisa slyly. "Someone who knows how to delegate. You could learn from him, husband."

I throw her a wry smile. "Yes, Raptor, you may appoint others to assist you, but as I said, keep the matter of the memory loss quiet until we return."

"Of course, Sire."

"The Queen and I will leave at once. Knowing who we are would only cause concern and unrest among the remaining residents. Besides which, I do not wish to spend another moment in this place, and I suspect my Chosen agrees with me."

"Fuck yes," says Louisa. "Let's go, right now."

I clasp Raptor's shoulders. "You will not be abandoned, I swear it. Even if we cannot restore your memories, you will be taken care of. For some of the prisoners here, this loss may be a gift in disguise. Whatever crimes existed in their past are expunged, and they can rejoin society in any role they choose."

"Thank you, Your Majesty."

Louisa squeezes Raptor's hand, gives him a parting smile, then follows me back down the length of the hall to the foyer and then out to the courtyard.

The eagerness to escape vibrates in every line of Louisa's body—she's practically running for the gates. With a laugh that changes into a low growl, I shift into one of my favorite forms—a silver dragon with scales of shining metal. I slither up beside Louisa and crouch low so she can scramble astride my neck.

When I first took this shape, it was difficult to speak. I've practiced a few times since then, so I'm able to ask, in the gravelly voice of this form, "Do you have a good grip, sweetheart?"

"I'm ready," she replies breathlessly.

I lunge forward, crawling up the outer wall of the prison and leaping from its turrets into the night air.

Louisa shrieks with delight, and it's all I can do not to let loose with a roar of triumph, of liberty. But that would terrify the denizens of Griem Dorcha, and they have been through enough.

The snow and ice disappeared when the Banríon perished, and the forest stretches below us in deep shades of purple and green. Overhead the dark sky arches, dotted with stars like snowflakes. At the horizon, there's a faint swathe of lighter color. The wind is cool, not frigid, and I angle my wings to meet it, riding its swells and surges.

Once we're high enough, the mountainous wind gentles, and I glide along a steady current. It's quiet up here as we sail softly toward the coming dawn.

"Tell me," I growl, in the voice of the dragon. "Tell me everything that happened to you."

So Louisa does. She tells me every detail—her anxieties, her fears, her faults, and her triumphs.

As she speaks, I begin to realize that I haven't understood her as deeply as I thought. I always viewed my wife as a bright, outspoken woman, boldly expressive, speaking her mind. She is outspoken, and yet she has kept so much inside. I had no idea she was doubting our marriage so deeply. I didn't realize how alone she felt, how she'd begun to wonder if I really loved her at all, or if I was merely the victim of her scent and Fate's hand.

"It's not fate, or destiny," I assure her, after she has finished her tale. "Or if it is fate, that's only part of the picture. I believe destiny has a hand in the meeting of every couple, but where they go afterward is up to them. And now that I remember everything, I can tell you with utter certainty that I *chose* you, every time. Not fate... *me*. Maybe I chose you for a slightly different reason in every case, but all the reasons were a part of you, and the cause beneath it all was *you*. Your essence, your soul. I would find you in any form, love you in any lifetime."

"Tell me," she says. "Tell me your side of it."

It has always been difficult for me to show emotion. My parents curbed overt displays of feeling, and I learned to suppress much of what I felt, to remain calm and collected, not only in the public eye, but among family. It was all I could do to confess my love to Louisa the first time, and it was difficult to speak to her again on the subject after she had rejected me once. Since then, I've maintained some restraint with her. Too much, I realize now.

When she asks for my part of the tale, I recoil inside at the thought of laying my heart bare. It's an instinctive reluctance, cultivated over time. But through the temporary suppression of my memories, some of that instruction from my parents has blurred and softened, easing its hold on me. Once I begin telling Louisa my side of things, I realize how freeing it is. How easy. How satisfying.

After what we've endured together, she knows me like no one else. Twice she has seen me broken down, stripped of my identity, captive and powerless—this time worse than the instance with Drosselmeyer. Yet she loves me still—admires my strength and resilience, she says. Though I've enjoyed respect from many of my subjects, others still mock me for allowing myself to be caught off guard and captured by Drosselmeyer. They think me weak, unfit to rule. But when Louisa expresses her admiration, I feel like those words alone could sustain me through centuries.

I talk to my wife for a long time, and she listens, though she plays with the edges of my scales as we fly. It annoys me a little, but I know she requires movement to focus on words for long periods of time, so I allow it. This is how we care for each other.

"What I'm taking from this," she says, "is that you need me to help you out more with the dull parts of rulership. You told me I wouldn't have to, but I *want* to, if it means we can spend more time together and if it will free you up for more relaxation. I understand there will be busy days when our time will be limited, and I can be happy with that as long as you learn to ask for help, and you stop trying to do everything yourself."

"And I'm hearing that you need me to prioritize your pleasure, to connect with you both physically and emotionally, even during busy or difficult times," I reply. "Stabilizing the kingdom and helping it prosper are worthy goals, but they are also never-ending tasks. I must learn to devote time to other things, to enjoy my life and to affirm my love in the ways that mean the most to you."

After a short pause, Louisa says, "And you'll let me help you? With the running of the kingdom?"

I hesitate, thinking of her boisterous ways, so different from the manners and customs of the Seelie Fae. We are not restrictive in the same ways that her father was, but we have a similar intolerance of things considered unacceptable in our society. Louisa's occasional coarseness, her impatience, her lack of attention at times—I can embrace it, but I'm not sure my people will. That's what this journey was supposed to be about—touring the land and letting the other Seelie fall in love with her like I did. But I chose to complete the most odious task first—dealing with the prisoners of Griem Dorcha—and now we must postpone the rest of our trip and return to Beannú.

Louisa's training was supposed to lead her into the royal guard and the Seelie army, where her vivid personality and her keen strategic mind would be most accepted. But can I trust her with affairs of state, with the sometimes delicate dealings of court politics?

I've been silent too long, and she speaks again, her tone stiff with hurt. "Lir. I want you to land right now."

"Do you have to relieve yourself?" I ask, even though I know that isn't the reason. I'm reluctant to have this argument with her now, when I thought we were understanding each other so well.

"Land," she repeats.

I spot a grassy bluff not far away and angle toward it. Immediately Louisa slides off my back and whirls to face me.

"I want to talk to you in your Fae form," she demands.

"I'd feel safer remaining in this one," I mutter. But the look in her eyes leaves no room for argument, so I transform into my usual self, shrouding my naked body in simple black robes.

"You don't trust me." Louisa's eyes are daggers, her voice a spear to my chest. "After all this—you still don't trust me."

"This isn't about trust, or even about us. It's about *them*. My people."

"Your *people*." She practically spits the word. "Lir, while you've been off purging the land of the Rat King's leftover minions and monsters, I've been *with* your people in Beannú. I've made friends. I've learned some of the culture. You seem to think I was lounging on pillows and eating sweets the entire time."

"I know you were training—"

"I did more than eat, train, and sleep. I began to learn. I discovered things I really don't like about the Seelie, and I also found many things to admire. I daresay many of the Seelie will feel the same way about me. I don't mind not being liked by everyone. But you—you're so afraid of failing, so afraid that I'll embarrass you, so terrified of not being loved, that you hesitate to even give me a *chance* to prove what I can do."

"I'm glad you were learning," I say quickly, before she can interrupt me again. "But the Fae live long, and as such our culture is far too complex to be absorbed in four months. You're asking me to give you responsibilities you're not ready for—"

"No!" she exclaims passionately, her fists clenched at her sides. "When did I say to give me *all* the responsibilities, or even specify which ones? I just asked you to trust me with *some*—with a few things, so I can help you."

My own frustration rises to meet hers. "You won't be of much help. Teaching you how things must be done will take twice as long as simply doing it myself."

"It might require more of your time at first, yes, but eventually I can take burdens off your shoulders."

"This isn't merely about minutes and hours and days. It's about expectations. The Seelie are used to a certain kind of queen. They expected me to choose a certain kind of partner."

"You mean *you* expected to choose a certain kind of partner." Tears glimmer in her blue eyes. "You think I don't know who you've always wanted me to be? I'm not that person. I will never fit that ideal in your mind. You've proved that you will choose to love me, but can you accept me? Or will you never stop trying to mold me into the mate you wanted?"

Counterarguments spring onto my tongue—rebuttals, protests, persuasions. I know how to argue, how to keep a debate going. I never relent until I feel that I've won.

What I don't know how to do is yield. I have very little practice with relinquishing my pride and permitting myself to be satisfied with something less than my ideals.

But ideals can be false, and pride can be deadly to love.

Will you never stop trying to mold me into the mate you wanted?

"Yes," I said hoarsely. "Yes. I will stop. Right now."

Louisa stares at me.

"I may have to stop again," I tell her. "I am deeply flawed, and as you confessed to me, so I will admit to you—I may slip back into old patterns, but I promise to strive against them, to reject them with conscious thought. To accept you, as you are. Mine, forever. You may not have been my former ideal, but you are my new dream. Being yours is a joy deeper than happiness."

Her anger softens, the tense lines of her face crumpling into something fragile and precious. Tears slip down her cheeks. She takes one step toward me.

"Forgive me," I whisper.

Then she's in my arms, and I'm holding her tight, gripping her as if someone might try to steal her away. My face is in her hair, my tears falling into the tangled golden locks.

"You can have everything," I say brokenly. "All the responsibilities you want."

She chokes out a tearful laugh. "Let's not get carried away."

"And if anyone dares to speak a word against you, I will—"

"No, Lir." She presses her hand over my mouth. "You will do nothing harsh or unreasonable. You will be the just, kind ruler you are, and you'll allow them to dislike me, because that is their choice. And we will continue living our lives, with or without the approval of others."

"Very well."

She removes her palm and kisses me, salty tears moistening my lips and hers. Then she pulls back again and tilts her head. "Maybe sometimes, if people are *very* rude to me, you can threaten them. Just a little."

"Thank you," I say fervently. "After all, they must learn to treat their Queen with the respect she deserves."

"Precisely. You're the only one who can disrespect me, with permission, in certain naughty situations." She surveys me, her pretty white teeth tugging at her lip. "How long will you have access to your dragon form?"

"A few more hours."

There are restrictions on my most powerful abilities. Unless the kingdom and I are in grave danger, I can only shift into my titanic form once every few months, and only for a short time. I can change into a dragon more often, for longer spans of time, but after each shift there is a waiting period of weeks before I can do it again.

I know why Louisa asked me that question. She has hinted a few times that she wants to explore my dragon form—even wants me to fuck her as a dragon. And she expressed curiosity about the sexual potential of my titanic form as well.

Since the danger to myself and the kingdom is so recent, I have control of both forms for a while. And we are in a remote part of Faerie, mostly uninhabited. There would be no better place to indulge my wife's curiosity.

I owe her this. We've been married for over a month, and together for a few months before that—though I was absent most of that time. She has been more than patient. Sexual freedom is important to her, and yet I've not delivered on my promise to experiment with her, to try *everything*.

I remember all my former inhibitions, my sober reluctance, the hectic schedule that kept me distracted, and yet none of that seems remotely important now. A rush of impetuous freedom races through my veins, and all I can think about is granting my Chosen those naughty wishes of hers.

"Sweetheart," I murmur, kissing her forehead. "I would like to show you a few things. As a dragon. If you're not too tired."

"I feel amazing, actually," she says. "I'm healed, refreshed... but Lir, you just got your memories back. You went through a terrible, invasive experience, not to mention actual torture. Are you sure this is the right time?"

She's being unselfish, thoughtful, kind, but my sweet girl can't hide the excitement in her voice. My heart nearly bursts with love for her.

"I'm sure," I tell her. "First, let's find a better spot for what I have in mind."

I shift back into dragon form, and with Louisa on my back I fly over the forest until I spot a small meadow, deep with soft blue grass and flecked with purple blooms. I land on all fours in the grass, my long silver tail slithering through the flowers.

Louisa climbs down from my neck.

"Dragon form first, or titanic form?" I ask her.

"Dragon, please." She's breathless, her cheeks rosy and eyes shining.

I roll onto my side, exposing the row of long, flat silver scales armoring my belly. The scales taper toward the rear, and between the last belly scale and the root of my tail, there's a seam in the flesh.

Louisa approaches slowly, and I shift my rear leg so she has an unobstructed view as I slowly extrude my dragon cock from its slit. It's nearly twice as long and thick as my usual one, and it's silvery gray, soft to the touch, with a ribbed texture. Its tip is more pointed and flexible than my Fae cock.

"The balls are internal," I explain to Louisa. And then I startle, because she's touching me. "Godstars, that feels... ahh..." I groan, and the ripple of sound rolls through my body, vibrating along my length with heightened intensity.

Louisa gives a soft gasp of delight. "It vibrates."

"So it does." I can't hide my own surprise. "I haven't done anything but piss with it, once. Can't very well touch it with these." I flex my thick, sharp claws.

"It's so thick," Louisa says. "I'm not sure I can take it this first time. But I want to try."

"I don't want you to be hurt."

"Lir." She stalks over to look in my dragon-face. "Stop. Enough wondering if you're going to hurt me. If I'm concerned about that, I will tell you. Understand?"

"Yes." My tongue slithers out between my jaws, as if it's craving the taste of her. I start to pull it back, but she only laughs, so I lick her cheek and her neck. She tastes even better than usual when I'm in this form, and my cock stiffens, pulsing. "I need those clothes gone, sweetheart."

She smirks. "As your Majesty wishes."

21

LOUISA

I've fantasized about being fucked by Lir's dragon form ever since I first saw it. And that fantasy is becoming real.

I'm naked, face-down in lush blue grass, with the fragrance of meadow flowers filling my senses. A beautiful silver dragon is lowering himself over me, his belly scales brushing against my ass cheeks. His cock is enormous, and I'm momentarily terrified, in the best and giddiest way.

I'm soaked, slick for him. But it will still be a tight fit, if it fits at all.

I adjust my position a bit, widen my stance, and reach between my legs to hold the flexible tip of the dragon's cock and guide it into my entrance.

"Slowly, Lir," I gasp as the massive cock nudges between my pussy lips. "Slowly."

He growls in answer, and the rumbling sound travels straight to his cock and sets it vibrating.

Never have I felt anything so intense, so violently exquisite. I shriek, my eyes rolling back. "Yes, yes! Again, Lir, please, do that again!"

Another rumble, and his cock vibrates against me. The tingling sensation floods my body, overwhelms my sensitized flesh.

"I'm going to come," I gasp. "Oh gods, Lir, fuck me, fuck me now!"

The dragon growls and pushes inside me.

Just the tip, probing into the slickness of my entrance, writhing deeper until the thickness of him stretches me wider, wider...

It's almost too much.

"Stop," I exclaim. "Stop, stop, give me a minute. Hold still, if you can."

The Lir-dragon makes a choked sound, and his cock pulses, but he waits.

Gradually I ease myself farther onto him. "It's just like taking two cocks at once," I murmur. "I can do this."

"My little Queen," he rumbles. "Such a good girl, taking so much dragon cock."

"Godstars," I gasp. "Keep talking like that, and I'll take it all."

"You like such things?" He sounds pleased, if a little embarrassed.

"I fucking love such things."

"Your pussy was made for thick dragon cock," he says, nuzzling my hair. "Let me fill you up, you luscious, beautiful woman."

Thus encouraged, I take him deeper.

The Lir-dragon shudders with need above me. He growls again, and as the vibration hits my pussy I move, fucking myself as deeply as I dare on his cock.

Glorious bliss rolls through my body, bathing me in a wave so strong I nearly collapse. "Fuck," I sob. "How does this feel... so perfect... godstars..." I rock backward harder, and with a violent groan the Lir-dragon hunches lower over me and begins to *fuck*. He ruts into me, roughly but not too deep—I'll be sore but I won't be damaged. He wraps one foreleg around me carefully, minding his claws, and he pins my body against his belly while he fucks me.

I melt into a blissful, softened mess of lust. My eyes are unfocused, my mouth open, my hair and breasts swinging as the dragon uses me. Only half of his length is inside me, and I've never been stretched so far or filled so completely.

With a guttural roar, he comes. His cock buzzes inside me, setting off a second blinding orgasm even as his cum surges into my belly. It's too much for my body to hold—he has to pull out, and the rest of his cum fountains against my bottom and thighs, dripping down my legs.

He rubs against me hard, with a final groan, then rolls over onto his side.

Weak and dizzy from pleasure, I crawl to him and settle against his foreleg, reach over to stroke his long, elegant muzzle with a shaking hand.

"We have to do that again sometime," I gasp.

Lir chuckles, his scaled sides surging with a laugh. "Indeed."

We lie there until the sun peeks over the tops of the purple and lavender trees. Once, I comment on the possibility that there could be monsters in this forest, but Lir assures me I'm safe. Nothing will dare disturb us.

After he has somewhat recovered, he changes from his dragon form to his titanic form—ten times his usual height, capable of crushing a whole section of the forest with one step. He lies naked in the meadow while I walk along the enormous planes of his abdominal muscles and wrap my arms around his immense erection. I rub my whole naked body against it, glorying in the debauchery of being next to that much cock. It's the strangest thing I've ever done, and Lir and I can't help laughing the whole time, especially when I lose my footing and roll onto his balls.

In the end he takes matters into his own hands, stroking himself while I watch. As I've imagined countless times, he releases a river of cum, forming a white stream that snakes through the meadow. It's disgusting, and absurd, and deliciously wicked, and I couldn't be happier, because he has thrown himself into this wild experimentation with whole-hearted good nature, not judging me for a single impulse, not even when I ask him to stick out his tongue so I can sit naked astride the tip. It's wetter and less sexy than I imagined, so after that, Lir returns to his usual size and we fuck against a tree, some distance from the river of cum that's slowly soaking into the ground.

"I love that you're being debauched and lecherous with me," I whisper as he pins me to the tree trunk, thrusting slowly between my legs.

"I have enjoyed it immensely." He kisses my mouth. "But perhaps we won't do the titanic cum thing again. I don't know what effect it might have on the local plant life."

I burst into laughter, and he grins, a dimple popping into his cheek.

This time, when we both come, it's transcendent. Joyful, and utterly satisfying.

For the first time in ages, I feel truly, deeply sated.

Lir conjures clothing for me, changes to dragon form again, and flies toward Beannú until he feels his dragon form waning. After landing, we walk until I'm too sleepy to go any farther. We could find a wayside inn, but we have no coin with which to pay, since our royal jewels and possessions are somewhere in Griem Dorcha. We were too eager to leave, and neither of us thought to reclaim any of it.

Once we're curled up together beneath a bower of flowered bushes, in a nest of conjured blankets, I can't stop my brain from rehearsing everything that happened to us and all the different outcomes there could have been. I keep shifting my position and rolling from one side to the other until Lir finally says, dryly, "Shall we keep walking a while?"

"No," I mumble. "I'll settle down eventually. It helps if I have something besides my thoughts to focus on. Will you sing to me?"

"I don't sing as well as Finias."

I half-sit up, propped on my elbow. "Stop comparing yourself to Fin."

"It's difficult not to," Lir says. "He's so flamboyant. And talented."

"But he doesn't have your powers. And even though I love him like a brother, I much prefer *you*."

"Why the fuck?"

"Did we not just learn this about each other?" I exclaim. "I love you because you're *you*. Enough doubts. Accept it."

He laughs a little. "Very well."

"I will stop comparing myself to Clara, and you'll stop comparing yourself to Finias."

"That's not an official bargain," he counters. "I can't promise, but I will try."

I settle back against the blankets, my shoulder against his, and I stare up at the latticework of pale flowering branches against the night sky. "There's no need for us to be jealous of anyone."

Lir shifts a little, and I know instantly what he's thinking.

"Would you like me to stop training with Dónal?" I ask.

Silence... then he says quietly, "Yes."

"Then I will. There are plenty of other warriors to train with."

"But he's the best."

"It doesn't matter," I reply. "Training with him isn't worth causing you pain or doubt. I'll find a replacement as soon as we return."

He sighs, and I smile, because there's relief in that exhalation. We trust each other, yes. But it's a kindness not to strain that trust too far.

Lir lifts his hand, and a flurry of tiny orange sparks rise from his palm to dance among the flowers above us. As I watch them, delighted and mesmerized, he begins to sing.

It's the melody I hummed to him in the cave, the first Fae song I've learned by heart. We danced to that song at the ball following our Chosen ceremony.

His voice is mellow, soothing to my overtaxed brain. The dancing orange lights begin to blur as my eyes blink heavily, slower and slower, as the voice of my Chosen eases me into sleep.

22

LIR

Louisa and I walk part of the way back to Beannú, but at last we stop at a royal outpost and reveal my identity. The startled guards offer us an escort back to the city, but we refuse it.

"All we need is a horse," I tell them, and they immediately give us the largest and strongest steed they have available, along with some food and coin.

Traveling alone gives Louisa and I the chance to talk for hours, and to pause for an impulsive fuck when the mood strikes us. We take a detour into a particularly pretty little valley, which slows our progress—but at last, we arrive within sight of the city. A fanfare breaks out the moment we're in sight.

"Our gate guards are overzealous," I mutter to Louisa, whose plump rear is nestled temptingly between my thighs. But she's looking to the north, at a pair of riders approaching the fork in the road. I spot tousled pink hair and the glint of sunlight on gauzy blue wings.

Finias.

Never in my life have I been so happy to see my cousin—not even when I first sought his help against the Rat King. We've grown closer since then, more like brothers, and I've missed him. Wild though he can be, he's steadier since he met Clara. He is strong, intelligent, and a formidable warrior. When he's around, I always have a loyal ally.

He and Clara ride toward us eagerly. They look a bit careworn, as if they're also returning from a long journey.

"Godstars, cousin," Fin exclaims. "What have you done to yourself? You look dreadful."

Perhaps I didn't miss him after all.

"You, sweet Louisa, look exquisite." Fin beams at her.

Clara is surveying us both, taking in our appearance with those keen brown eyes of hers.

Louisa shifts uncomfortably under her sister's gaze. "Our trip did not go as planned."

"We have much to tell you," I add.

"Much to tell?" Fin taps his chin. "Did you, perchance, forge into Unseelie territory to rescue a kidnapped maid and steal the Tama Olc from the hands of a powerful spellworker? Did you fight the mindless droves of the Heartless, fool the entire Dread Court with glamours, and aid in the destruction of that devious Queen, the Eater of Hearts? Did you celebrate the newfound freedom of the entire Unseelie kingdom and send a human girl safely home?"

I gape at him, utterly shocked.

"Clara!" Louisa exclaims. "You little minx! You said you were 'visiting a friend'!"

"We were. Fin has friends everywhere," Clara replies.

"If 'friends' is a term loosely defined." Fin gives us a broad grin.

"Apparently we have a long night of storytelling ahead." I urge our horse into a faster walk. "We'll need sustenance. Once we get to the palace, I'll call for food."

"And wine," Fin adds. "Plenty of wine. I'll make dessert."

"Please," says Louisa fervently. "I haven't had a good, thick slice of cake in ages."

Once we have bathed, we feast. Both the cake and the wine are plentiful, and despite the tragedy in our tales on both sides, none of us can find it in our hearts to be sad.

"What do you think of the denizens of Griem Dorcha, Fin?" I ask. "Can their memories be restored?"

Fin winces. "I think not. I will consult my books, and a few friends, but as far as I know, such magic is both rare and permanent. But good news—the spell around the prison should have already evaporated by now. We'll have to test it, of course. We can find some terribly boring courtier, tie a rope to his waist, and trot him along the road toward the prison, then pull him back and question him to see if his mind is intact. If not, it won't be any great loss." He tips his head back and pours wine into his mouth.

Clara sputters a reproachful, "Fin!" but she's laughing, and so is Louisa.

"I vote we send Bergis," suggests my wife. "He's the dullest courtier I've met."

"Oh gods, hush!" Clara whispers through a giggle. "The servants will hear you, and they'll tell him you said so."

"Might teach him to be a bit more vivacious," Louisa answers. But she sobers then, and turns to me. "What will you do if their memories can't be restored?"

"We'll take care of them, as I promised," I tell her. "The Crown will provide all they need to begin new lives."

"The guards we were traveling with," she says, staring into her wine cup. "I think most of them were killed or eaten. We'll have to find out for sure, and tell their families."

I slide my fingers over hers. "I'll meet with their families myself, tomorrow, and explain the situation."

"I'll go with you." She meets my eyes and nods firmly.

Despite the gravity of the task we'll be facing, my heart lightens. This is still my Louisa, and yet she is even more lovable. Strong enough to help me bear the burdens I must sometimes carry, as the king of this land.

Fin is watching us, his yellow eyes sparkling. "You two seem—better. Not that you weren't good before, but Louisa, you've never seemed more like a queen, and Lir—clearly a gigantic stick has been pulled out of your royal ass—"

I lunge for him, and he jumps lightly out of his chair and flies up beyond my reach.

"Fuck that," I growl, and I pull off my shirt as silver wings burst from my back. I leap into the air and chase Fin across the ceiling, something I would never have dreamed of doing a few weeks ago.

"Ho-ho!" crows Finias. "So the King deigns to have fun now, does he?"

"Not fair," Louisa shouts. "We can't fly! We want to have fun too!"

Clara jumps onto her chair and begins pelting my cousin with sugarplums from a golden bowl on the table. Louisa squeals her approval and starts throwing food as well—cheese wedges, tarts, biscuits, berries—until Finias and I relent and descend, covered in dinner scraps.

Finias picks up Clara and whirls her around, and I take Louisa's face between my hands. She and I don't spin, or dance, or laugh. We look at each other, with the weight of everything that was done to us, and the promise of everything we will do. No matter what we've told Fin and Clara, they can never understand what we endured, nor can we fully grasp their journey. But together, we are a family.

And as I kiss Louisa's soft mouth, I think of the day I went to the garden to read a book, and was waylaid by Drosselmeyer. Little did I know that wretched experience would lead me to the greatest treasure of my life—my bride, my mate, my Chosen.

more books by
REBECCA F. KENNEY

The DARK RULERS adult fantasy romance series
Bride to the Fiend Prince
Captive of the Pirate King
Prize of the Warlord
The Warlord's Treasure
Healer to the Ash King
Pawn of the Cruel Princess
Jailer to the Death God
Slayer of the Pirate Lord

The WICKED DARLINGS Fae retellings series
A Court of Sugar and Spice
A Court of Hearts and Hunger
A City of Emeralds and Envy
A Prison of Ink and Ice

A Hunt So Wild and Cruel

The PANDEMIC MONSTERS trilogy
The Vampires Will Save You
The Chimera Will Claim You
The Monster Will Rescue You

For the Love of the Villain series
The Sea Witch (Little Mermaid retelling with male Sea Witch)
The Maleficent Faerie (Sleeping Beauty retelling with male Maleficent)

The SAVAGE SEAS books
The Teeth in the Tide
The Demons in the Deep

The IMMORTAL WARRIORS adult fantasy romance series
Jack Frost
The Gargoyle Prince
Wendy, Darling (Neverland Fae Book 1)
Captain Pan (Neverland Fae Book 2)
Hades: God of the Dead
Apollo: God of the Sun

The INFERNAL CONTESTS adult fantasy romance series
Interior Design for Demons
Infernal Trials for Humans

Printed in Great Britain
by Amazon